A Thousan

A Thousand Blended Notes

musical tales of three cities

Ronald Watson

Roseberry Press

British Library Cataloguing in Publication Data
A catalogue record for this book is available from the British Library

ISBN 978-0-9933825-0-5

Typeset in Dante by Amolibros, Milverton, Somerset
www.amolibros.com
This book production has been managed by Amolibros
Printed and bound by T J International Ltd, Padstow, Cornwall, UK

This book is lovingly dedicated to Isabel, my partner in time, archivist, advisor and proof reader without whom many of the events recounted in its pages would never have happened and the accounts of them would have been much less reliable.

I heard a thousand blended notes when in a grove I sate reclined…
William Wordsworth

Foreword

Ron, like me, is a Yorkshireman, though a more northerly one than I. He can still lay claim to that title despite his long exile south-east of the Wash; and, to be sure, his loyalty and affection have never wavered, from his transplanting to Norfolk, through the many years there, up with which he has put, enjoyably though, and productively.

Indeed, over and above his bread winning he has carved for himself a significant niche in the world of music, church choirs and organs, and perhaps most importantly, as a composer. His first piece I met, the *Suite for Leeds* was followed by many others – *Jubiläum*, birthday present *90 Bars* (music ones) – one for each year I had accumulated, *Eucharistia*, and the rest, all chronicled in these pages. And I can take this opportunity of registering my indebtedness for his kindness in taking on the computerisation of a symphony I had written and transcribed for organ. It was entirely his idea, a huge task and greatly appreciated.

His association with The Reverend Fred Pratt Green is noteworthy, as is his editorship of *The Journal* (published by the Norfolk Organists' Association) with his often pointed utterances. His untiring work with choirs, here and abroad, attests to his devotion, his constant enthusiasm and his joy in the cause of music.

Francis Jackson

Contents

List of Illustrations

1) *St John's Church. The oldest church in Middlesbrough.*

2) *Conrad Eden at the console of Durham Cathedral c. 1965.*

3) *Winning the Hugh Longstaff Memorial Trophy at the North of England Musical Tournament in Newcastle upon Tyne.*

4) *Dr Francis Jackson c. 1965. Picture used with permission.*

5) *Revd Dr Fred Pratt Green.*

6) *St Giles Church, Norwich.*

7) *Kevin Bowyer autographs the author's programme after performing Rievaulx at St Mary's Standon.*

8) *With June Nixon at Lambeth Palace after her receiving her Lambeth Doctorate.*

9) *Dr Gerald Gifford after performing Homage to Buxtehude on his own harpsichord at St Thomas's Church, Heigham, Norwich. L to r Brian Lincoln, the Very Rev'd Alan Warren, RW, and seated Gerald Gifford.*

10) *Sine Nomine singing in the gardens of the Kloster Mariensee near Hanover.*

11) *With Gillian Ward Russell, Tim Patient, Dr Arthur Wills and David Dunnett at the author's seventieth birthday celebration in Norwich Cathedral.*

12) *Isabel.*

Cover illustration provided by Martin J Cottam.

Introduction

This is an account of my musical experiences in three cathedral cities where I encountered church music of the highest order and acquired my love for it. It also traces my musical journey from being a parish church organist to being a published, performed, recorded and broadcast composer.

Throughout my journey I have been fortunate to encounter just the right people at just the right time, people who opened doors, gave me a helping push along the way and championed my music.

I hope that this book helps to encourage any who feel that they have something to say worth hearing and not to be deterred in pursuing their goal – whatever that might be.

First Encounters

I was born in Thornaby-on-Tees in the short reign of Edward VIII. Thornaby is geographically in Yorkshire but was identified mostly with Stockton-on-Tees, which is just across the river Tees in County Durham. Indeed it did not get its charter to become a Borough until 1892 before which it was known as South Stockton.

My childhood home was always full of music and my development in it went parallel with my development in all the other facets of human experience. I learned to read words and I learned to read music; my feet learned to walk, my fingers learned to play. My mother taught piano pupils at the house, quite a lot as it happened. From 4.30 in the evening until 8.30, eight pupils let themselves in at half-hour intervals through our front door (never locked until last thing at night), and into the front room. I heard the lessons of raw beginners who were brought into awareness by *From The Beginning* by E Markham Lee, *Diller Quaille Companion Pieces* and *Thumer's New School of Studies*, to very advanced pupils tackling Sinding's *Rustle of Spring*.

Just by hearing this process I developed an awareness of what was musically right and what was wrong and at a very young age would go to the piano, an Erard upright, and pick out tunes. This Erard piano was well worn. It had been bought by my grandfather for my mother when she was a young girl as he wanted her to become a concert pianist. I'm not sure that would ever have been a realistic prospect, as not only was she very short in stature but her hands were so small that she could not stretch an octave. That aside, she was forbidden to do any housework and made to practise eight hours a day.

By her early twenties she was a sought-after teacher in Middlesbrough which brought her into contact with Edmund Gallettie, with whom she fell in love and whom she would marry in 1915, giving birth to his son, my half brother Ray in 1916. Edmund served in the Black Watch and was killed in 1917 and his name appears on one of the memorial panels at the gates of the town's Stewart Park. The death of her husband brought an end to any hope of my mother becoming a concert pianist and from then on she had to use her musical skills to earn enough money to provide for herself and her young son. Apart from teaching she also played in small orchestras primarily in the music halls. She continued studying and obtained her ARCM at the age of thirty-two.

Whilst she could play nothing by ear and could not improvise in any way, she could play almost anything at sight, which was just as well as the music hall acts presented the orchestra with copies of their music on the first afternoon of the show with the first performance in the same evening. The artists carried these scores around with them from venue to venue and some were very much the worse for wear and often difficult to read. Her involvement with the music hall brought her into contact with all the stars of that genre of the day: Cavan O'Connor, Adelaide Hall, even Charlie Chaplin who appeared at the Middlesbrough Empire when she was playing there. It also brought her into contact with my father. My father was involved in silent films behind the scenes producing sound effects and playing appropriate music on gramophone records, which was not otherwise being provided by the small ensemble that included my mother, on the audience side of the screen. There was during my childhood still a large collection of these 78s in the cupboard under the gramophone and

I used to play them. I remember playing the overture to *Zampa*, *The March of the Caucasian Chief* by Ipolitov Ivanov and Haydn's *Toy Symphony*, one of my very favourites. I shall never forget hearing this for the first time whilst eating a soft-boiled egg. Just as I had filled my mouth, the toy trumpet played its three-note fanfare which I found so funny that I spat out all of my mouth's contents. I then tried to finish subsequent spoonfuls of egg and swallow them before the little fanfare re-occurred as each time it made me shake with laughter.

Also amongst the record collection was one at 80 rpm of Dame Clara Butt singing 'Abide with Me'. There were several of Count John McCormack, a favourite of both my father and my, by now, twenty-five-year-old brother.

My father occasionally went to the piano to amuse himself. He could play only by ear but very accurately. He could not read music at all and refused to learn. One item in his repertoire was *Simple Aveu* by Thomé, which he pronounced with no trace of French as something approaching Simpler Voo. Whilst his own skills were as an artist, he was very discerning when it came to music and knew the worthy from the unworthy, which he referred to as tripe. He was firmly of the opinion that Strauss waltzes were not a patch on those of Waldteufel. He hated chamber music which he referred to as 'po music', neither could he stand warbling sopranos which he declared sounded like some woman with her foot trapped. He always couched his criticisms of music in humorous terms. He was a bit of a wag. ('It looks like rain,' he would say, peering out of a nearby window, as someone was pouring cups of tea that were somewhat on the weak side. Those who knew him knew what he meant.)

I did have an in-built desire to conduct and I don't quite know where that came from, but I do know that as a very young child, pre-school, I would stand on a small armchair facing over the back of it and conduct the orchestral music I was playing on the gramophone. (I never did, in fact, conduct an orchestra but would feel totally at home in front of a group of singers in later life.)

Occasionally at home I would hear my father's twin sister sing accompanied by my mother. My Aunt Dorothy (Auntie Dot) had a fine voice and took the lead in several productions of Gilbert & Sullivan and other musical comedies and such like. I also heard my mother and a fine local 'cellist, Robbie Knox, play together, one of their favourite items being 'The Swan' by Saint-Saëns. And later, my mother would accompany me when I was learning to play the violin.

When my mother was working at the local theatre in the music hall and pantomime seasons, I would go to the shows and enjoy the small but polished orchestra assembled for the purpose under the direction of their Spanish conductor, Don Ernesto. Each variety show would begin by the orchestra assembling in the pit and Don Ernesto making his entrance from the rear of the stalls resplendent in white tie and tails and carrying his baton. Once on his podium he would turn to the audience, acknowledge their applause, then turn into position and strike up the overture. Don Ernesto occasionally came to tea at our home and would play our piano very heavily which my mother hated. 'He's a good player but I wish he wouldn't bang,' she would say after he had gone. My mother was very outspoken about those holding what she termed bogus degrees and diplomas, which she scathingly referred to as 'the cap and gown brigade'.

This was reinforced on one occasion which began when she and I were in our sitting room in the quite late evening when there was a knock on the door. 'Who can this be at this hour?' she muttered as she went to answer it. I heard a man's voice and my mother taking this mystery caller into our front room where she did her teaching. Some few minutes later she let the visitor out and came back to sit with me. It seemed that this gentleman, a violinist, had come to request my mother's services as accompanist in a diploma examination he was entered for that very weekend. He had left my mother the piano parts of the pieces he was to play, which she agreed to learn, and meet him at the examination venue the following Saturday at the appointed time. There would be no opportunity for them to play the pieces together, which my mother found somewhat unnerving and not very satisfactory. Being totally professional, she practised hard and mastered the accompaniments. On the day she returned home after the examination in a state of fury and disbelief. It seems that the candidate played very inaccurately both as regards the notes and the rhythms, yet, when he had finished, was congratulated warmly by the examiner who handed him his AVCM diploma there and then. This had all been a far cry from the rigour of my mother's examination for her ARCM and she was disgusted. Her disdain for bogus degrees and diplomas rubbed off on me and has remained with me to this day.

Quite early on, my mother tried to teach me to play the piano from music but because I was un-cooperative, she arranged for lessons for me each Sunday morning from Muriel Thomas who had gained her LRAM under my mother's tutelage. And so my journey at the keyboard had begun.

At a very impressionable age I saw the film *The Magic Bow*, which was purportedly the story of Paganini with Stewart Granger a most unconvincing violinist. This made me decide that I must learn to play the violin and one was obtained for me. From about the age of eleven I went to Stockton weekly for violin lessons with Harry Russell, someone with whom my mother had played in orchestras and smaller ensembles in earlier days. I made good progress and seem to remember getting to sixth position. Whilst I would never reach the heights of Paganini I'm sure I was a whole lot better than Stewart Granger. I had also seen *Song to Remember*, the story of Chopin, which kept my enthusiasm alive for the piano. However, as 'O' levels approached, the violin was abandoned forever and the piano kept merely ticking over.

I also fantasised from an early age about being a great composer, seeing a piece of music, a masterpiece on the music desk with my name on it. My earliest attempt was a song called 'The Robin's Song', for which I wrote not only the music but the words as well. Judging by the handwriting (in green ink!) I would be about eight or nine:

> *Verse 1: Little robin's back again, when the snow is on the plain.*
> *Verse 2: To a house old robin comes as he gets a plate of crumbs.*
> *Verse 3: Then he turns and hops away in the snow so thick*
> *doth lay.*
> *Verse 4: Then the wee bird gives a sigh; then he goes into the sky.*

It is childlike in every way yet I remember insisting that my mother send it off to Edwin Ashdown for publication. They must have had a good laugh when it arrived but nevertheless wrote a polite letter returning the manuscript, pointing out with regret that it was not quite what they were looking for at that time. I also remember getting my Auntie Dot to sing it with my mother providing the accompaniment.

My first involvement with a choir was at Middlesbrough High School where I was selected as the third in order of preference of three boy sopranos, the other two being John Jackson (the best) and Jack Tweddle (a close second). Quite why we were singled out I cannot remember but John Jackson had a lovely voice and got to sing solos. Choir performances mainly centred around Speech Day and the school concert, and I remember sitting on the tiered seating near the organ in Middlesbrough Town Hall along with the rest of the boys, with some masters who sang tenor and bass, and performing several songs, the only one of which I can remember being 'Of Neptune's Empire let us sing'. So much for that. Singing was the only musical activity at the school. Anyone wishing to learn an instrument, or indeed study any aspects of music, had to have private lessons.

One such was my dear friend Michael Addison who was a very gifted pianist and came to my mother for lessons. I remember vividly one evening his mother coming to see my mother to tell her that Michael wished to give up the piano. They were both very upset about this but his mind was made up. However, Mrs Addison need not have fretted as Michael took up the organ and began lessons with the Organist of St Paul's Church, Thornaby, Harold Maddock. In the later school speech days, always held in Middlesbrough Town Hall, Michael would contribute a couple of items on the Town Hall organ. I remember him playing the *Toccata* from *Suite Gothique* by Boëllman and a newly published piece by Harold Maddock, *Jour de Noces*.

Early development

In addition to the subjects in which I would take 'O' levels as part of the set curriculum, I decided to take 'O' level Music and, as the school did not offer tuition in this subject, I went along for private lessons with Harold Maddock. Harold was one of that band of amateur organists and choirmasters who kept the music in parish churches going to a very commendable standard. In keeping with others in this field he worked during the day at something totally removed from music, in Harold's case, as a modest clerk in the ICI chemical works. However, when his work colleagues were passing spare moments doing crosswords or filling in their football pools for the weekend, Harold would be ruling manuscript paper and putting his mind to problems of harmony and counterpoint at which he was very proficient. He had gained his LTCL diploma and was a very competent organist. He was also the very first person I ever met who had had a piece of music published, *Jour de Noces,* cleverly based on the initials of the couple to be married. He lived with his wife in a humble bungalow. They had no children which, my mother once told me, was a great source of sadness to Mrs Maddock.

I was involved at St Paul's, Thornaby as a server and was taken by the organ and enjoyed Harold Maddock's playing. Sometimes the organ would be played in Maddock's absence by David Rutter who was a Deacon at St Paul's (Thornaby) and was a very competent organist. (He later went on to become Precentor at St Paul's Cathedral in London and ended his career at Lincoln Cathedral. He also taught me to play chess in the Young Communicants' Club which met on Friday evenings).

Michael Addison was by this time very proficient and also deputised in Maddock's absence with me alongside watching. I too was beginning to be interested in learning the organ and decided to approach Harold Maddock for lessons. I sidled up to him one Sunday morning after the Eucharist service as he stood waiting at the bus stop. I told him of my success with 'O' Level Music and thanked him. I then asked him if he would take me on as an organ pupil. His response knocked me for six. He certainly wouldn't. In his opinion I had too great a propensity for trusting to luck and he couldn't see me making anything of it. I was very shaken, disappointed and bewildered, and reported the same immediately to my mother who was furious. Over the years she had passed several pupils on to Mr Maddock for the theory side of their examinations and she told him in no uncertain terms that he owed it to her to give me at least a chance. And so I began lessons with him, which I did take seriously, and I think demonstrated that his earlier impression of me was not entirely accurate.

After 'O' Levels I gave the sixth form a try but wasn't happy going down that path and decided to enter the world of work. My first job was with the local building and civil engineering firm of Tarslag Ltd. Here I would encounter another pivotal figure, though not a musical one, in my first boss, Don Hannan. I had taken the job of Junior Clerk in this company for no better reason than that it was on offer. I could just have easily ended up in a chocolate factory, a flour mill, anywhere. I was without any direction in my life regarding any sort of career and it was Don Hannan who suggested that I begin to study Building and contrived for me one day's absence each week to attend the local technical college on condition that I worked on Saturday mornings. It was he that instilled in me some self-belief and changed me from being totally rudderless to having a career path. He had noticed that two of my 'O' levels were Music and Art, the latter he also sought to have me develop, he himself being a gifted artist.

I did have access to the organ in St Paul's for practice where I learned Bach's *Eight Short Preludes & Fugues* and progressed to more difficult works roughly in the order they appeared in Novello books 2, 3, 4 etc. I did, however, purchase book 8 and set about learning the great *G major* and the *Fantasia & Fugue in G minor*. I also bought *Variations on an Original Theme* by Flor Peeters which was a fresh idiom I was thoroughly taken with. I used to play this to a young lady admirer, who rewarded my efforts by allowing me to walk her home.

On going to Durham University, Michael Addison became organ scholar at Hatfield College and studied with the cathedral organist, Conrad Eden. One afternoon Michael took me to Durham and sought Conrad Eden's permission to let me up into the organ loft during Evensong. The Durham loft must be one of the most cramped there is, so there was I virtually right on top of the console watching everything that went on and being enthralled by it. I also remember having experienced nothing like this ever before, the volume and variety of sound and wonderful reverberation in that magnificent building. The voluntary that afternoon was Franck's *Third Choral* which I immediately purchased, learned and have played countless times in my years as an organist. That afternoon was a pivotal moment.

In the years to come I would often be in the organ loft either at Durham or York for Evensong and was struck by the seeming telepathy that there was between organist, clergy and choir. There was no closed circuit television in those days and in each case the organist was tucked away out of sight and with no means of contact with what was going on below. Conrad Eden sat with the organ loft curtains behind him drawn, and Francis Jackson sat, in those days, on the south side of the screen, in a sort of cabin. When it came to the final voluntary he would draw back a pair of shutters over his head so that he could hear the full effect of the organ. During the service, notes were given and music begun seemingly without any cues. The organ loft was a separate, private world.

On one occasion Michael Addison suggested that I should enter the North of England Musical Tournament which was held in Newcastle-upon-Tyne. For this I had to prepare two pieces, Bach's five-part *Fantasia BWV 562* and a piece by Charles Wood out of *The Little Organ Book;* this I did under Mike's guidance. As my working week included Saturday mornings I needed to ask for a Saturday morning off in order to play in this competition. Don Hannan confided in me many years later that he did not wholly believe that I was going to enter an organ-playing competition but gave me the benefit of the doubt. I won and took the trophy into work the following Monday morning partly of course to show it off but also as proof that I actually had played in the competition.

This pattern of life was brought to an abrupt but not unexpected halt by my being called up for National Service. I opted to serve in the RAF for three years and after initial training was fortunate to be posted very near to home. My first posting, at Longbenton near Newcastle-upon-Tyne, enabled me to be at home most weekends and also to practise in the local church which was only a few hundred yards from the camp. Getting into the church in the winter months tested my nerve as it involved walking through a dark graveyard and letting myself into a totally dark church. I think extinguishing the lights as I left was even more scary; I was always relieved to be back where there were street lights. I did quite a lot of practice there and remember learning Bach's *Toccata & Fugue in D minor BWV 565* during that time along with the *Giant fugue BWV 680.*

Shortly before my period of National Service, Harold Maddock had moved to Middlesbrough and occupied the post of Organist and Choirmaster at St Aidan's Church which had a very new two manual Binns organ. I had some lessons there with him. Then while I was away he moved on to St John's, the oldest church in Middlesbrough, where I would eventually succeed him, he having suffered a stroke shortly before my release.

Immediately after my release in 1957, aged twenty-one, I helped out for a short time at St Luke's Church in Thornaby for Revd Joe Penniston whilst their organist D Emlyn Prosser recovered from a stroke, until news filtered through that, as Harold Maddock would never be fit enough to resume his post there, St John's were looking for an organist. This coincided with D Emlyn Prosser being deemed well enough to resume his duties at St Luke's and so I was able to accept the offer of the post at St John's. Out of a sort of courtesy but mainly out of curiosity, I attended a service at St Luke's for which Prosser was playing. It was unbelievably awful. Mr Prosser may once have been a competent musician but that had not been the case for quite a while and those days were clearly well and truly over. And so I went to St John's, Middlesbrough, and to my Durham experiences would begin to add involvement with York.

The St John's years

My first encounter with a church choir had been as a server at St Paul's Church, Thornaby. I didn't sing in it but was very much aware of it and of my mother's cousin John (Jack) Bashford who simply shouted everything in a raucous voice. I could not understand at the time why he wasn't asked to leave but learned in later life that there was more to belonging to a church choir than the ability to sing.

At St John's I cut my teeth as a choirmaster with a full robed choir made up of young women, boys and men. Some of the boys were very good and others were totally devoid of any singing or musical talent whatever and were there for other reasons. The adult members had been in the choir for many years and some of the boys were sons of church families. I succeeded two very experienced and revered choirmasters and I am sure there was much to make allowance for in my own inexperienced efforts to fill their shoes. However, I was deemed good enough to prepare and direct a group of singers from the Deanery who augmented my own choir to sing at a Eucharist in York Minster. The girls did not take part in this; it would be many years before girls occupied cathedral choir stalls. The service was accompanied by the then assistant organist, Ronald Perrin, but I got to play the voluntary, the Bach *Five Part Fantasia,* under his watchful eye. By this time the console was in its present position at the east of the instrument.

For some time the choir at St John's enjoyed good music-making and put on anthems and carol services of a good standard. Conrad Eden once attended an Evensong as RSCM Commissioner and in his report declared himself to be very pleased with what he had heard.

Previous organists at St John's had, as an annual pilgrimage, taken the choir to York for the Diocesan Choral Festival and I was strongly pressed to continue this. I cannot remember the procedure but we were duly enrolled and informed of the music that was required for the 1958 gathering. The choir were totally convinced (particularly the girls) that the organist at York, Dr Francis Jackson, was the greatest thing, not only since sliced bread, but more significantly since God had said, 'Let there be light.'

One of my acts of preparation for this was to attend 1 Minster Court, York, for a briefing with Dr Jackson and I was permitted to take along with me Frank Baker, one of my basses and a close friend. We were shown into a ground-floor room that housed a piano and an array of seats for the choir leaders. I don't remember there being too many there but there were certainly present several ladies of advancing years who spent most of the time drooling over the effortless playing of examples by the great man, particularly the first page of Basil Harwood's 'O How Glorious is the Kingdom' with its demi-semi-quavers. After the briefing, which included careful guidance on how to manage the pointing of the psalm, we dispersed, but for some inexplicable reason Dr Jackson walked Frank and me to St Helen's Church to see a new organ there and invited us back for tea.

For the service itself the large numbers of sopranos, altos, tenors and basses, each choir wearing their own robes, entered the Minster at different points, processing up the side aisles, across the rear and down the centre aisle to their places singing 'All Glory Laud and Honour'. On a podium in front of the organ screen stood Dr Jackson nobly trying to keep us all together – an impossible task.

(Nothing quite as ambitious was attempted at the equivalent event in Durham where choirs were asked to be in their places in the cathedral by a particular time.) Due to the vastness of the building, those near the west end were hearing what had been sung up to two seconds previously. The organ was being played from a detached console on the north side but the organ itself was, of course quite a bit further away. Even when we were all in our places it became apparent that getting such a large choir to sing as one voice in a building of the scale of the Minster was never actually achieved but the experience was most moving, inspiring and unique.

At one of these festivals Francis Jackson's hymn tune 'East Acklam' was used for its intended purpose to the words 'God that madest earth and heaven', which would be of considerable significance for me many years later. For a later festival the advance notice stated that a new work was being prepared for the service by Dr Jackson based on the harvest hymn 'Fair waved the golden corn'. A second notice some weeks later indicated that a substitution had been made as 'the seed did not germinate'.

No visit to York was complete without a browse in Banks Music Shop when it was at the bottom of Stonegate. They had EVERYTHING! 'Do you have an organ transcription of Smeltinski's *Metamorphoses on the Axolotl mating call?*' 'Yes sir, which edition would you like?' (Slight exaggeration, but that's how it seemed.)

Eventually the choir at St John's started to run into troubled waters. Factors contributing to the decline in the satisfaction derived from choral music-making were various. One was that the Vicar, Harry Richardson, saw the choir as a refuge for any young boy he thought St John's should take under its wing. These boys were not from families who were regular attenders (not that that in itself is a problem), but were often missing from practice and services for the usual reasons, days out at the seaside, looking after younger brother, forgot! One boy in particular whom I was asked to take was totally tone-deaf. His attempts to sing a note at any pitch resulted in a noise not dissimilar to that made by a seal as it pops its head out of the water. He did, however, love it, even though most of the time I insisted he stay silent. He had no socks, no handkerchief and one piece of footwear, a pair of plastic sandals which he wore whatever the weather. His family were in poor circumstances and the Vicar was 'working on them'. Other boys, however, became young men, lost their voices and then went off to university or National Service. The young women got married and moved away. My friend Frank Baker went off to Selwyn College Cambridge, took holy orders and later became Precentor at Derby Cathedral. One stroke of good fortune befell me with the arrival of a new curate, Michael Walter, who as a boy had sung at the Queen's Coronation. He wanted to train the boys, declaring that there was no such thing as tone-deafness and that he could produce results. I was happy to let him try.

The Vicar held very firm views on certain matters. He would not conduct a burial for anyone who had committed suicide, of which there were two instances during my time there. He was none too keen on the presence within the choir of young women and he detested Midnight Mass at Christmas. He also decreed that no fees would be charged for funerals and I played gratis for quite a few in my time there.

St John's vicarage was very much a male domain (except for the lady housekeeper). The Vicar made it quite clear that he and the Curate, Jack Elstone, were a team and wherever one might go as the incumbent the other would go in a supporting role. Young deacons who came onto the strength from time to time had it made clear to them that lady friends were not allowed.

A favourite Bishop of Whitby at the vicarage was the bachelor Philip Wheeldon. A framed autographed photograph of him adorned a small occasional table in the vicarage sitting room. At one of my weekly meetings with the Vicar to settle on the hymns and psalms and other music, I noticed that the photograph was face down on the table which I pointed out to the Vicar thinking that it had fallen over accidentally. 'I know,' said the Vicar, 'it's intentional.' It transpired that Bishop Wheeldon, who had been translated to Kimberley and Kuruman, had committed matrimony and was out of favour.

His successor was the enormous George D'Oyly Snow (father of the television presenter Jon Snow), a towering figure even without his mitre! When he visited St John's he always waited at the back of the church to listen to the final voluntary and as I made my exit always had appreciative words to say. Snow's years as Bishop of Whitby coincided with the launch of the Austin Mini. The press had a field day when the Bishop decided to be photographed in a Mini. In order to accommodate his great size, the driver's seat of the car had to be moved so far back that the Bishop found himself looking out of the off-side rear window. Much was also made of the difficulty that he experienced attempting to extricate himself from the vehicle.

There were certain features of an organist's life in those days which have now disappeared. My daytime practice was often interrupted by the need for one of the clergy to carry out the churching of a woman who had recently given birth. Weddings were concentrated on the period in Spring immediately preceding the new tax year as couples got a full year's tax rebate by tying the knot at the end of a tax year in which they had been taxed as single. This meant that on the last Saturday of March I would find myself playing for a succession of weddings as couples came to the altar at regular intervals during the day. I would arm myself with sandwiches and a flask and spend most of the day on the organ bench, nipping into the adjacent vicarage when there was the chance, to use the lavatory. At the end of the day I would leave the church with my pockets bulging.

As a routine part of every Sunday, I visited Harold Maddock after the morning service and, despite the fact that his stroke had deprived him of the use of his right hand, we played the 'great' organ preludes and fugues of Bach on the piano with Harold playing the pedal part with his left hand. We also listened to records and talked about matters musical. It was on his gramophone I first heard the recording of Evensong from King's College Chapel, Cambridge which included the Evening Canticles by Stanford in G and Francis Jackson's *Toccata in B minor*.

In this period my own development continued. I started to have lessons with the organist of St Barnabas Church, Middlesbrough, Reg Denyer who had been a pupil of Bairstow and was a thoroughly good organist and general musician. The organ at St Barnabas had three manuals, the first such instrument I had played. Reg introduced me to many fine works; Sonatas 6 and 8 of Rheinberger, three of Bach's Trio Sonatas, Stanford's *Fantasia and Toccata*, Flor Peeters' *Ave Maris Stella* and the *Modale Suite*. Several years later, attending a Bank Holiday organ recital in Norwich Cathedral, I noticed Reg in the audience. I had not seen him since my Middlesbrough days. I sat next to him and asked him, 'What are you doing in Norwich?' 'I live here,' came the reply. He had moved down from Tees-side and been appointed to the post of organist at St Andrew's Church in Norwich, a post he held until his death.

One of my burning ambitions was to obtain a reputable diploma as had my mother. And so I approached Conrad Eden at Durham Cathedral for lessons with a view to taking my ARCO diploma. Not only was Durham a lot nearer than York but my friend Michael Addison had put in a good word for me. My lessons with Eden were enjoyable though they had their bizarre moments. On one occasion he stopped me in the middle of a piece and asked me what I thought of anyone who filled a milk bottle with petrol and threw it at a shop window. Eager to say the right thing I said that I thought it was terrible. 'So do I,' said Eden, 'now where were we?' At one lesson I had just got started with the Bach *Prelude in C BWV*

545 with a diapason chorus. 'Oh no,' he said, drawing a single flute, 'play it on this so we can hear what is going on.' This I duly did. At the next lesson I drew the same flute and began the piece. 'What on earth are you doing?' he said. 'This needs quite a lot of organ,' which he set up and made me start again. One of my lessons had to be cancelled because someone had committed suicide on the high altar and the Cathedral had to be re-consecrated.

An essential part of passing the playing part of the ARCO was (and still is) the competent playing of the keyboard tests, sight-reading, transposition and reading from an open score, competent meaning at the correct speed and without any mistakes. There was no grading in the marking of these, a candidate could either play them exactly as written or not. In my lessons with CWE I received no guidance on how one might approach the tests – I simply practised these myself. CWE could just 'do them' but probably didn't understand how to teach anyone else the skills.

I got along very nicely with CWE though I know there were those who didn't, not least his assistant, Cyril Maude. I always found him encouraging and accommodating. He would let me on the organ if I asked, as I did one Easter Monday evening. He let me into the cathedral, departed and locked me in to play to my heart's content. At one point I decided to air the Tuba and the big pedal reeds. I drew the stops but there ensued nothing but silence – he had them on a separate switch, the location of which was known only to him. When he came to let me out I told him I had tried to use the reeds but without success. He disappeared out of sight for a brief moment, leapt on the bench and played the C S Lang *Tuba Tune* with everything blazing. On another occasion he let Mike and me into the Cathedral after hours armed with reel-to-reel tape recorders which we set up in the choir. We spent the evening taking turns to play things as the reels did their reeling. Eden left us alone for a little while but returned later on and sat in the nave listening. At the end of the session he himself played Flor Peeters'

Concert Piece twice and *Final* by Jesus Gueridi. All of this I still have on tape which somehow, one of these days, I'll get transferred to a more up-to-date recording medium. Having noticed that Francis Jackson was a MusD FRCO and CWE was a MusB ARCO, I once was gauche enough to ask him if he'd ever thought of taking his FRCO. 'Why should I play to them?' he retorted quite bluntly. The RCO did, some years later, confer an honorary fellowship on him and I went down to Kensington Gore to see him receive it alongside another recipient, Simon Preston.

He once took me round to Harrison's works where had been invited to try out an organ destined for St Clement Danes, the RAF church in London. It was interesting to watch him put it through its paces. He gave the opening recital on that instrument once it was installed and the reviews of his recital were glowing. The critic chose to express regrets that Eden was rarely heard outside the Durham area. I believe he did not do 'the circuit' to the extent that other cathedral organists did and it wasn't until much later in my life that I heard from another reliable source that the likely reason was that the Durham post was very well paid and that it was possible that Eden did not have the same necessity to supplement his earnings as did his peers. He certainly didn't overcharge for lessons; when I told him I had passed my ARCO I received a bill for 7/6d (about 35p in today's terms).

He also confided in me that he had opened an organ in a Roman Catholic church in Darlington which had put him off opening organs in RC churches ever again. It seems that he was all ready to begin playing when a verger scuttled up to the console and asked him to hold fire whilst the organ was blessed. This had involved a small procession to the console and the priest liberally sprinkling holy water over everything. He claimed that, in addition to himself, his music on the desk and all the keys were saturated and he had had to attempt to dry the whole area with a handkerchief before he could begin.

One incident which caused great mirth amongst the musical fraternity in the North East was that of Conrad Eden appearing in court and being bound over to keep the peace. This had arisen because, driving home one evening and being still a long way from home and very hungry, the Edens stopped at a hostelry which had a sign advertising meals. On entering the establishment they were told that the kitchen had closed for the day and that there was no food available. The infuriated CWE returned to his car, and grabbing the sign threw it into the boot and drove away. An account of this featured in the local press, a cutting of which was sent to me by a friend who had written across the bottom – 'and the rich he hath sent empty away'.

Pursuit of the ARCO led to a further encounter with Dr Jackson. I had passed the oral and paperwork sections of the examination at first go thanks to the excellent grounding I had had with Harold Maddock, but success in the playing eluded me. At a second attempt in The Barony Church in Glasgow on a bitterly cold January morning in 1967, I could see huddled in the centre of the nave the two examiners W (Bill) Lloyd Webber and Francis Jackson. There appeared to be no heating in the church and the two examiners were wearing scarves and, I think, fingerless gloves, while their breath appeared as a white vapour. It was just as cold at the organ console. I did not satisfy the examiners on that occasion which puzzled me somewhat as indeed it puzzled Conrad Eden who thought I was definitely up to the standard, though I don't recollect ever having played the tests for him. On my return home I decided to approach Dr Jackson with a view to him hearing me play and offering any suggestions as regards any shortcomings which I might address to succeed.

This resulted in my making the fifty-mile journey to York where, at 1 Minster Court, I was shown to an upper room in which was a two manual pipe organ. I duly played the two set pieces to Dr Jackson who declared them to be up to standard. His only comment was about John Gardner's Chorale Prelude on 'Down Ampney'; 'It's a long way from Down Ampney,' he observed wryly and then put me at my ease by saying, 'I meant the piece, not your playing.' Having insisted that I must be fully prepared for the tests, which he thought was probably the reason I hadn't pulled it off, he walked across to the minster with me and told me that all I really needed was a bit of self-belief. I gained the diploma in London the following summer.

In 1967 I had the Forster & Andrews organ in St John's rebuilt by J W Walker & Sons. Money had to be raised for this and a range of initiatives were undertaken including an attempt to interest the then Prime Minister Edward Heath, himself an organist of some ability, who did send a contribution, and the most popular singer at the time, Val Doonican. I asked him to donate one of his sweaters but this he declined to do. He did, however, send us an autographed LP which we auctioned at one of our fund-raising events.

The organ builder suggested that we should get Dr Jackson to open the instrument once completed and that recital took place on 8th February 1968 (my birthday as it turned out) and I acted as page turner for the great man as he played, amongst other things, his *Toccata, Chorale & Fugue* from his own manuscript which, I commented, deserved to be printed in gold, an observation that gave him some amusement and which he still recalled in his nineties.

In celebration of the rebuilding of the organ I arranged four recitals, the second to be given by Conrad Eden and therein lies a tale of one of the most complicated episodes in my life as an organist. At one of my lessons with Conrad Eden I told him of the rebuild. I probably said something like, 'You must come and play it when it is finished,' to which he replied that he would love to. What I hadn't realised was that he had understood this to mean that he was to give the opening recital, which had never been my intention.

As Dr Jackson's recital approached I had a large poster made, complete with photograph of the recitalist, advertising the event which was prominently displayed in the entrance porch of the church. One evening I had a phone call out of the blue from Conrad Eden saying that he would be in Middlesbrough the next morning and would like to come to see the organ, and a time was duly arranged. Fortunately I was in a job which had a company car and plenty of freedom to come and go and so I got myself rapidly to the church just before Eden was due to arrive and removed all traces of anything that made any reference to Dr Jackson's opening recital. It worked. Eden came, ran his fingers over the keys, examined the stops, expressed his delight at the organ and how much he was looking forward to opening it, and left. He was no wiser.

The Vicar offered to invite each of the recitalists to a meal before their recitals with a particular special guest, the former Headmaster of Middlesbrough High School, W W Fletcher, who was something of an eccentric but an avid fan of organ music. On the evening of Dr Jackson's recital the chosen few sat down to a delicious meal prepared by the Vicar's housekeeper and then sauntered over to the church for the recital. So that was that.

For Conrad Eden's recital some four weeks later, the Vicar once again invited the same people to the pre-recital meal. I had by this time explained to him that Conrad Eden thought he was opening the organ and that everyone should be briefed not to mention Dr Jackson's recital or that the organ had already been opened. The weak link in this plan was W W Fletcher who didn't seem to understand what was afoot. True to form at several points during the meal he began to say how much he had enjoyed Dr Jackson's recital but was skilfully diverted as one of us suggested that he might be referring to a recently broadcast recital. Despite one or two similar uncomfortable moments, miraculously nothing was discernible from anything that was said over the meal which let the cat out of the bag. As we moved across from the Vicarage to the church for Conrad Eden's recital we noticed that Eden had parked his car on the paving between the the two buildings and I noticed that there was someone sitting in it. It was Conrad Eden's wife. As we walked within feet of the car there was no acknowledgement from our recitalist but the Vicar said to him that he should have said his wife would be with him and she would have been welcome to dine with us. I don't remember Eden's exact words except that he thought that his wife was very content. She sat there throughout the recital.

For a third recital I invited back the last but one Organist and Choirmaster at St John's, Donald Hammond, and to complete the sequence gave the last recital myself. In each of these recitals I included a choral interlude engaging local singing groups. One such was The Columba Singers who had done very well indeed on the BBC's *Choir of the Year* programme. Their founder and conductor Matthew Parkin (someone else with a daily job far removed from music), hand-picked the singers and drilled them to as near perfection as one ever gets. They were drawn from all walks of life, none was a professional singer but each had a desire to sing a good standard of repertoire and sing it well. I envied Matthew's situation given the difficulties with running the church choir I was encountering, outlined above. He had no problems with motivation, tone-deafness, poor attendance or any of the things church choirmasters had to contend with on a weekly basis. He could also explore the secular repertoire.

As a Contracts Manager for the local building firm Charles Tennet Contractors I was put in charge of the building of an extension to St Paul's Church, Stockton. It occurred to me that it would be a nice idea if, wearing my other hat, I gave an organ recital when the work was complete and invited my friend Alan Barber to take part with his choir, which he duly did. I often accompanied the Deanery Choir, which he directed, and learned much from the way he worked with them. I had first encountered Alan when he came to St Paul's, Thornaby, to succeed Harold Maddock. Unfortunately there was some unease between Alan and David Rutter and Alan's first tenure of that post turned out to be very short-lived. Happily he returned to St Paul's some years later when he had a much longer and very successful stint.

The most comprehensive organ in the area was in Middlesbrough Town Hall. The Town Hall had, in the early part of the twentieth century, been the cultural hub of the region. The Borough Organist, Felix Corbett (1861 – 1940) was, according to my mother, quite flamboyant as he slid up and down the bench with his tails flying. When my friend Alan Barber left the post of Honorary Borough Organist at the Town Hall he took into safekeeping lots of music which he knew would be sent to the incinerator if he didn't intervene, amongst which were symphonies of Widor and Vierne which had been Corbett's copies. Vierne's were Nos. 1 2 3 & 5 and on the title pages of 1 2 & 3 are Vierne's signature extending his good wishes, which seems to indicate that they were good friends. The fact that Corbett's pencilled registrations are scattered on the pages of Nos. 1 and 3 but no fingering or footing on any except two left-hand fingering indications on the Final of No.1, leads one to believe that he must have been good enough to play this difficult music, coupled with the fact that it is unlikely that Vierne would have had such an intimate friendship with a less than competent musician. There were also two simple piano pieces composed by Corbett: *Jeu D'esprit,* Caprice for Pianoforte and *A summer day* also for pianoforte published by Warren & Phillips, London.

Corbett was above all an amazing impresario and brought to Middlesbrough the most famous musicians of the day. There is a Corbett Memorial window in the Town Hall bearing the names of some of the great artists that came to perform there, names such as Rachmaninov, Melba, Paderewski (Paddy Roosky as the locals had it), and many others. My mother recalled attending these Corbett Concerts and seeing all the wealthy arrive in their carriages in their finery. She also saw the mad Vladimir Pachmann who performed at the piano with two carers alongside in case he leapt into the audience. He was a great Chopin interpreter but talked to himself and the audience the whole time he was playing. When I was quite young, though old enough to sit still, my mother took me a piano recital in the hall by Pouishnov, which I remember being very impressed by.

The local Organists' Association engaged several leading organists to give recitals in the Town Hall in my time. In addition to the two nearest cathedral organists there were others from further afield, Arthur Wills from Ely, who played the final section of Liszt's *Ad nos ad salutarem undam* and a piece of his own which I didn't quite get the hang of. There was also the very gifted Philip Dore from Ampleforth. I remember from Francis Jackson's recital a newly published *Toccata* by Gordon Philips which I obtained straightaway and enjoyed playing. I also remember that Conrad Eden played Vierne's *Carillon de Westminster* and was somewhat disappointed that he did not use the organ's chimes. I should have known better than to expect anything the least bit gimmicky from this discerning musician.

Being at St John's brought me into contact with two of my former schoolmasters, 'Chuck' Hewson and Ross Stobbart who were churchwardens there. In both of their subjects I had been useless, in Hewson's case it was Physics which I simply didn't get, and in Stobbart's case, woodwork. (If I were to describe myself as cack-handed it would be too complimentary.) However, I did take some delight in demonstrating to those gentlemen, inter alia, on Sundays that there was something I was good at! This reminds me that Ross Stobbart was the only one of my schoolmasters whose Christian name I actually knew. All of the others were known by their nicknames. *Spike* – Cherry, English, *Sam Slab* – Mathematics (a Mr Smith – how he became Sam Slab goodness only knows!),

Shags – Mr Francis, Latin, *Taffy* Evans, also Latin, *Poppa* Plant, History. The Headmaster W W Fletcher was known simply as *The Boss*.

Whilst I was in the North East, EMI brought out their Great Cathedral Organ series of LPs and not surprisingly I bought both Durham and York. Conrad Eden's was very adventurous with Karg-Elert's *Homage to Handel* and *Variations on a Recitative* by Schoenberg and Francis Jackson's included Willan's *Introduction Passacaglia & Fugue*.

A few incidents during my time at St John's are worthy of a telling. For a short period I was the proud but rather impecunious owner of a cream MG PB, two years older than myself. It had one persistent shortcoming in that the dynamo, mounted vertically at the front of the engine, spewed oil outward and backward and itself became so gunged up with oil that it ceased to function. There was on sale an oil seal which was not expensive and which, it was declared, was extremely easy to fit. Having acquired this device, I started early one Saturday morning to fit it. I donned my filthiest clothes and dived down into the bowels of the bonnet to remove the necessary bits in order to insert the seal. I was filthy; my hands and arms black with oil. I was unshaven and having touched my face on and off looked not unlike a chimney sweep. When I was in the midst of this the telephone rang and it was the Vicar enquiring if I had remembered the wedding, due to start in a little under half an hour. I was mortified, carless and six miles away. Our next door neighbour had an even older Austin 10 and was a bus driver. I ran next door and begged him to drive me to the church. He agreed but drove in a painstakingly slow manner, stopping frequently to give meticulous hand signals. En route I was frantically trying to clean myself up using an old towel I grabbed as I ran out of the house. We arrived at the church and the wedding was by then in progress and I had to pass through the congregation looking totally disreputable on the way to the organ. I was in position in time for the first hymn and played for the rest of the ceremony without incident. Having played them out, however, I was very reluctant to make my own exit from the church given my disgusting appearance and so skulked out of sight until they had all gone. It transpired that the Curate had managed to switch the organ on and draw a stop, and having done so played them in to the Bridal March with one finger and quite a few wrong notes.

Some months later after Evensong I was invited to join a couple from the choir at a nearby pub for a drink where they had arranged to meet two of their friends. To my horror the two friends turned out to be the couple whose wedding I had only partially played for. I was, of course, full of apologies and it was all laughed off as quite a quaint occurrence.

On another occasion I was in the church practising quite late into the evening, and in a few moments when I was not actually playing I heard someone lock the main entrance door. I scuttled the length of the church to the door to discover that I was locked in with no means of letting anyone know of my plight. Then I remembered that the main fuse board for the church and the vicarage was in the vestry, the vicarage being only a few paces distant, so I decided to throw all the switches. This had the desired effect and within a very few minutes I heard the lock turn in the main door and the footsteps of the Curate approaching down the aisle wielding a torch. Once I knew my exit was assured I returned all the switches to the ON position and revealed myself. Again, this was laughed off, though I suspect that the Vicar and Curate must have been very irritated.

The boys in the choir at St John's lived mostly in circumstances in which treats were rare. I did, along with the Curate, take them on trips away, to Durham and York and in the winter up onto the moors for some sledging. Charles Tennet Contractors were most generous in allowing me to borrow a van to transport the boys on these jaunts. I was particularly thrilled once when we learned that there was to be broadcast (on the radio of course) a *Songs of Praise* from Middlesbrough which would be recorded in St Barnabas Church. Choristers from all of the Middlesbrough churches were invited to be part of this and the prospect of being on the radio thrilled my boys beyond measure. On the evening of the rehearsal it was ensured that all the boys were seated in the first five or six rows of pews, mine I remember were quite near the front. The organ was to be played by Reg Denyer and the singing was conducted by Stan Burnicle, a significant figure in the musical life of the town. The rehearsal went well and everyone went home contented and looking forward with eager anticipation to the actual broadcast. When we arrived at the church on the appointed evening all of the boys' rows were already full and there were no seats at all left for my St John's boys. I protested to Reg and to Stan but they had other things on their minds and were not prepared to remove the interlopers. Consequently my boys were turned away to their total dismay and disappointment and my disgust. I was, and still am, sickened at the thought that there could be such one-upmanship associated with an act of worship. The meek may well be destined to inherit the earth but in the meantime they can sometimes get a very rough deal.

The mother of one of the choirboys wanted him to learn to play the piano and asked the Vicar if he thought I'd be willing to teach him. When putting this to me, the Vicar was concerned that he didn't think the family could afford very much by way of tuition fees. Having got the message, I agreed to teach young George Witherly for nothing so long as he didn't waste my time and was fervent in his practising. After only a few lessons George asked me if I liked eels, as one of his pastimes was fishing for eels in the muddy banks of the Tees estuary. I told him that I had never eaten eels but would be interested to try some with the result that when he came for his next lesson he had with him a shoe box containing a couple of dead eels. I was duly instructed in their preparation which involved splitting them open and removing the innards, then chopping them into pieces about two inches long and boiling them. Until then I had only heard second-hand how slippery eels were, which fell very short of the reality, which is that they are virtually impossible to hold, let alone handle. I approached the preparation by liberally sprinkling flour on to a chopping board and coating the eels' slippery surface in it. I managed, and having carried out the whole procedure ate the result which I can best describe as interesting without being exciting.

Asked at the next lesson how I had enjoyed the eels and not wishing to pour cold water on George's generosity, I said how much I had enjoyed them, which turned out to be the wrong answer. From then on I was presented at each lesson with a shoe box containing up to half a dozen eels. Getting rid of them became something of a challenge. On one occasion I took the shoe box into the typing pool at my place of work and left it on one of the typist's desk. Within seconds of my exodus from their office, screams and shrieks emanated from within as one of the ladies had opened the box and in a state of shock dropped it and sent the eels slithering all over the floor. (They were dead, of course, but slithered all the same!) I had to go in and scoop them up into the box and remove it and its contents as far away as possible. There inevitably came a time when I asked George to stop bringing me the eels and assured him that no gesture as a token of my feeless lessons was necessary.

I did have an organ pupil at St John's, Martin Penny, who was clearly very gifted and destined to become a very good organist. It was not long before I suggested that he should have lessons with Conrad Eden and I put a good word in for him in that quarter. At his last lesson with me in 1968, he presented me with the manuscript of a short organ piece, *Fanfare*, which he had written for me as a token of gratitude for my organ lessons. The piece was clearly influenced by Kodaly's carol 'All men draw near', which appeared in *Carols for Choirs 1* published by OUP in 1960.

One very happy outcome of my time at St John's was the result of a bit of inadvertent matchmaking on my part. One of my young colleagues at Middlesbrough Town Hall, Mike Turver, began to accompany me the short distance to St John's at lunchtimes where I went to practise. He showed a keen interest in the organ but also expressed a desire to sing in the choir which meant him cycling from Billingham in all weathers on Sundays. In the choir he met Kate and Cupid got to work. In due course they married and have had a long and happy marriage with the blessings of children and grandchildren. It would come to light many years later that Mike and I were distantly related through the McNeil side of both our families. Another of the basses in the choir, Albert Russon, took the trouble to teach me to swim. We met at Middlesbrough Baths early on several mornings during which time I got the hang of it. He married one of the sopranos, Sheila, and I had the privilege of becoming godfather to their first son, Peter. The family emigrated to Canada whence I lost touch with them for many years.

Finally I must recount the most bizarre occurrence of all, which even when I recall it after all these years gives me goose pimples. During my time at St John's I got married and my first daughter arrived. We had her christened at St John's. One afternoon I was practising and I heard much bumping and thumping going on downstairs in the vestry. I came down the stairs into the vestry to see what was going on. There was a large square table in the centre of the vestry and it was on this particular afternoon laden with old registers as a new safe had been purchased and they were relocating all the records from the old safe into the new one. These registers went back many years and as I stood and looked I noticed that the uppermost register on the corner nearest to where I was standing was dated 1916. I opened it to see beautiful copperplate entries on each page and wondered what had happened on the 8th of February 1916, some twenty years prior to my own birthday. I was astounded to see there the entry for the baptism of my half brother Ray who had been born in 1916 on 20th January. I had had no idea that he had been baptised in that church where half a century later I would hold the post of Organist and on the day exactly twenty years before I would be born. For want of a better word I found it spooky then and still do.

In 1968 York Minster was diagnosed as having serious structural weaknesses and a massive programme of work was begun to prevent its collapse (under the supervision, ironically, of Sir Bernard Fielden from Norwich, whom I would later encounter swimming vigorous lengths of the bath in Norwich's St Augustine's swimming pool). One of the effects of this was that the organ was encased in a huge plastic sheet and as there was a huge hole under the tower, the entrance through the choir screen was achieved by crossing a temporary bridge. I attended a recital by Francis Jackson whilst all this was going on and the programme comprised only two items, Bach's *Prelude & Fugue in A major BVW 536* and the whole of Messiaen's *Le Corps Glorieux*. I was sitting in the nave and witnessed the exit of a substantial number of people who had had enough of this avant garde piece well before it was finished. One by one they tramped very audibly over the bridge. It was all a bit embarrassing. I am not sure to what extent the recitalist was aware of this.

During all of this time I was writing piano music and settings for the St John's choir and sending them off to publishers, never with any success. I did, however, begin my organ *Toccata* and showed an early draft to CWE who thought it had merit and would have played it if it had been longer. (Once in Norwich I revisited the piece and it became my first ever published organ piece. It later found favour with Kevin Bowyer who recorded it and gave it an honourable mention in the IAO Millennium Book complete with a reproduction of the first page.) I also wrote a hymn tune, *Walter*, to the hymn 'Jesus shall reign'. I did nothing to bring this tune into use but was gratified to learn some sixty years later that Fr Michael Walter, whose name it bears, still had a copy and had used it several times over the years during his ministry. A carol, written for St John's choir and dedicated to Kate and Mike Turver, 'The Maker of the sun and moon', eventually found its way into print in 2004 when it was published by Escorial Edition.

In 1968 circumstances surrounding my occupation made it necessary for me to find another job. I felt something of a square peg in the commercial and cut-throat world of contracting and sought something which I felt would be more in tune with my personality. I noticed in *The Sunday Times* an advertisement for the post of Senior Lecturer at Norwich City College in exactly those aspects of the construction process that I was experienced in. And so I applied and was appointed. I think the fact that I was an organist may have swayed at least two of the interview panel in my favour, certainly one of whom was the Principal, Dr John Croft who knew St John's, Middlesbrough. I was on the road to Norwich.

Norwich City College – the springboard

I joined the staff of Norwich City College in September 1968 as a Senior Lecturer in the Department of Construction. I was very fortunate in joining the College at the same time as Howard Burrell who had been appointed to develop musical studies there. One of the first things Howard did was to form a chamber choir. Another stroke of good fortune was that Dr John Croft had been quick to note that I had the ARCO diploma. It was he who engineered that Howard should use my keyboard skills with the City College Singers for whom the first task was to prepare a Christmas programme for the annual Carol Service in Norwich Cathedral, for which I would play the organ.

I acted as accompanist for the choir at rehearsals and in concerts and learned an enormous amount from Howard Burrell about preparing choral music and about the choral music repertoire. I accompanied Britten's *Rejoice in the Lamb*, *Festival Te Deum* and much else besides and when I was not required at the keyboard would sing bass in such pieces as Kodaly's *Matra Pictures* and *Jesus and the Traders* (fiendishly difficult piece!), Stanford motets, madrigals and part songs.

Howard was a keen footballer and on one occasion broke his leg just prior to the departure of the choir to Bristol where it was due to give two concerts. At the last moment, once it became clear that Howard would not be able to make the trip, it fell to me to direct the choir in Bristol which I duly did. Directing such a well-drilled and talented choir gave another boost to my ambition to have a chamber choir of my own.

The College were invited, as part of Norwich's twinning activities with the city of Rouen, to send the college choir and so it was that, as their accompanist, I went with them to Rouen where we were guests of the much larger choir the Chorale Voix Unies under the direction of Gérard Carreau. This association was fostered by Howard Burrell and in due course the French choir paid a return visit to Norwich and performed at the College.

Whilst on my first visit to Rouen with the City College choir, I was introduced to Jean-Louis Durand, organist at the fine church of St Maclou. I was shown the organ and being in need of something to play asked if he had any Bach handy. He produced from his music cupboard a book of Chorale Preludes, some of which I would have been happy to play. However, having selected one, I was taken somewhat aback by the fact that the tenor melody line was written in the tenor clef. Rather than make a mess of it, I opted simply to extemporise and sample the various stops. I was invited some years later to give a recital in that church and went over independently to do it. Some years later on a visit to Rouen I learned that the organ I had played had been replaced by a Kern organ of which Jean-Louis was extremely proud.

Another encounter at City College was with Ralph Bootman, an organist and dabbler in organ restoration who, having heard of my arrival, got me to give a recital in the disused Chapel-in-the-field Congregational Chapel where there was a fine three manual Norman & Beard instrument. The building at that time stood empty but a key could be obtained and the organ could be used. I remember playing Bach's D major *Prelude & Fugue* and Messiaen's *Apparition de l'église eternelle*. In 1972, prior to the demolition of the chapel, the instrument was moved to Somerleyton. Ralph also got me to join the Norfolk Guild of Organists as it then was.

Ralph was Organist at St Giles Church in Norwich, an imposing building with beautiful wisteria bushes adorning the boundary. When he developed back trouble he asked me to stand in for him at St Giles Church until he was fit to return. As it transpired, Ralph never returned and I remained at St Giles for twenty-two years. There was a choir there when I went, ninety per cent of whom relied on being picked up and brought to the church by one adult member in a van. Sadly, the gentleman van driver was involved in a tragic miscarriage of justice which led to his being suspended from his job, which meant him absenting himself from St Giles and eventually moving out of the district. The choir, fatally depleted, ceased to exist. This suited me very well as, after my experience at Middlesbrough and my ambition to have an independent chamber choir, I was not really interested in the fruitless struggle to rebuild a choir in that place.

At about the same time I was approached to get involved in the music of the village church in Drayton where I lived. For some reason I took a choir practice in the church and became acquainted with John Thaxton who was one of the leading members at that time of the Norfolk Opera Players. He and a few others of the Opera Players wanted to explore the a capella repertoire and John approached me with a view to directing this small group in four-part unaccompanied folk songs, madrigals and such like. This was the beginning of the Lyrian Singers. The first sing-through took place in the sitting room of my not very large home in Drayton but, as the word spread and more people were keen to join the group, rehearsals began on a regular basis in the local school.

After several rehearsals it was clear that the choir would need some sort of an administrative structure to deal with obtaining music, annual subscriptions, engagements, dress and all such matters as choral directors will be very familiar with. At my suggestion, a committee was formed and one of the bass singers, a retired Squadron Leader who had taken part in the Berlin Airlift and was at this time a practising solicitor, was elected Chairman. John Thaxton, who served as Treasurer, and I considered ourselves as co-founders of the choir. I was happy to leave the administrative matters to the committee but insisted on having the final decision when it came to matters of repertoire and all other musical considerations. I had achieved my ambition of following in the footsteps of Matthew Parkin and had, in my assessment, a chamber choir equal in standard to his Columba Singers.

Meanwhile Howard Burrell moved on from Norwich to Hatfield and his successor, Ron Boote, was not interested in maintaining the link with the Chorale Voix Unies, about which I felt very sad. Making sure to get Ron Boote's approval, I approached Gérard Carreau with a view to arranging exchanges between his choir and the Lyrian Singers, a suggestion that was eagerly taken up and resulted in many years of cross-channel music-making in Norwich and its twin city and an enduring personal friendship. I composed two pieces for this ensemble, a carol 'Chantons Noé', which was published in Lyon by A Coeur Joie, and 'My beloved spake', originally published by Oecumuse but which is now in the catalogue of fagus-music.

So it was not long before I arranged to take the Lyrian Singers to Rouen where we gave joint concerts with the Chorale Voix Unies under Gérard Carreau's direction. We chartered a Dakota aircraft and flew from Norwich to Deauville, thence went by coach to Rouen. This link flourished and within about two years we were invited to join our French friends and a choir from Rouen's other twinned city of Hanover in La-Charité-sur-Loire where we had a glorious week singing together and giving concerts in beautiful churches in the area. As part of this I gave an organ recital in the church in La Charité which was something of an eye-opener. The recital was scheduled to start at 8 pm and as the church clock struck eight there was no one in the church. I came down from the organ loft and enquired of the verger where everyone was.

'They will come,' he said. Sure enough from about 8.20 people started to arrive and by half past the church was full. At the end of my recital I was summoned to the front of the church to receive applause and be presented to the Prefect of the region. (As I made my way past the verger he tried his best to compliment me in English. 'Ah Mister Watson, zat was terribul.' Fortunately I knew enough French to realise he didn't mean 'terrible' but 'terrific'.) The report in the following day's newspaper of the recital mainly dealt with who was in the audience. It seems that in some areas people go to such events primarily to be seen and have it reported that they were there. Scheduled starting times for concerts were regarded with considerable flexibility.

The link with the Herrenhäuser Chorgemeinschaft from Hanover was developed and exchanges between Norwich and Hanover occurred at regular intervals over several years, which included a second visit to La Charité. At one concert in the church in La Charité was a Dutch gentleman who expressed an interest in forming a connection between us and his choir in Amsterdam. We exchanged contact details and soon a trip to Holland was planned, flying from Norwich in a chartered aircraft. This, unfortunately, was at the time of a fuel crisis in this country and our charter of the plane had to be cancelled. The link with the Dutch, it seemed, was lost, but some years later would re-emerge.

On a separate occasion whilst on holiday in La Baule in Brittany, I went to hear a blind local organist in the nearby town of Guérande. At the same recital was a German couple from Berlin who, as it turned out, were staying in La Baule very near to where I was. Addresses were exchanged and before long the Lyrian Singers visited Berlin where we sang on one of the local radio stations and gave concerts in churches. The choir from Berlin visited Norwich on two occasions.

It was the policy of the Lyrian Singers not to exceed five voices to a part which meant that numbers always remained around twenty.

New singers, and replacements of those who moved on, were made by personal contact and resulted in several people joining us from the City College. I tended not to audition prospective new members but to invite them to attend and take part in a rehearsal. This would highlight pretty accurately their suitability as choir members as I took note of how their voices blended, how well they sight-read and, just as importantly, how well they fitted in with the rest of the group. However, at one stage I decided that perhaps I ought to audition, which led to one of the most bizarre situations I have ever encountered. I auditioned a middle-aged lady who sang like a lark at her audition and was thus taken on. From that moment onward she sat through rehearsals without ever opening her mouth, not what is required in a small choir where everyone should be able to hold his or her own part. Despite several attempts to get to the bottom of this, she remained a complete passenger until she finally left. There was pressure on me not to exclude her from the choir as she loved the social contact and was of a sensitive disposition, thus membership of the choir was a tremendous therapy for her but there was never anything in return. My thoughts went back to John Bashford and some of the boys I had in Middlesbrough who were in the choir for all the wrong reasons. The Lyrian Singers was very much a learning experience for me and one decision I had made, to be democratic, would prove to have been unwise.

Due to personal difficulties and internal politics within the choir, I parted with the Lyrian Singers in 1978. The issue of choir apparel had arisen and there were two opposing opinions and it was decided to put the matter to a vote. I expressed the view that if there had to be a deciding vote I should cast it. The Chairman insisted that he should have the casting vote and pointed out to me that I was not at the helm of the choir, he was. I was very disappointed by this and his stance resulted in my deciding to resign. It had never been my intention to be an employee of a choir I had formed. It also marked the end of a what I had regarded as a very valuable friendship. The choir continued successfully for some further years under the direction of Ina Bullen.

However, there were certain things in life I could not live without and by now, working with a chamber choir was in my blood and it was not long before I formed Sine Nomine. Slowly, members of the Lyrian Singers came back to sing with me, and with Sine Nomine I continued the former foreign links and visited Rouen, Berlin and Hanover, forming a new link in 1986 with the Hoeksteen choir in Amsterdam which grew out of the contact in La Charité all of those years earlier. We were joined on these foreign jaunts by David Morgan, an accomplished organist and colleague of Ron Boote.

Running a choir can be a bit of a bumpy ride, however. Choirs are made up of human beings who are, after all, only human. A small chamber choir is particularly vulnerable to the sore throat or other eventualities which can reduce one part to as few as two voices, or even one. Each concert is a nagging worry until the conductor sees the whites of the eyes of all the singers safely at the venue, and there are some tales to tell about that. I had one tenor who, for quite a long period, would get lost on the way to an engagement; lost in the snow in the country lanes around Lyng and Elsing, or quite simply having gone to the wrong place. In Berlin on one occasion one of our number, a young woman, was held at Friedrichstrasse Station, an East-West crossing point and given no explanation. Fortunately, she was eventually allowed back into the West, again without explanation, but that did not matter. The relief was indescribable.

The most depressing place in which we ever performed must surely have been Gressenhall (a former workhouse and now a rural life museum) when it was still a home for the elderly. The finest places we have sung in must be the cathedrals of Norwich, Ely, Peterborough and St Edmundsbury in this country and wonderful churches and cathedrals across the Channel.

Choir members can become like a family and as such are deeply touched by happy and sad events which befall fellow members. We have shared births and marriages, bereavements and in one case a member killed in a car crash weeks before we were due to go to Amsterdam.

I always vowed that the end of my choir directing days would come before I became a spent force and standards started to plummet. I have always believed that standards of amateur ensembles can be brought remarkably close to professional standards and that when that happens the rewards are truly wonderful. One thing I have learned is to know the limitations of the choir and not to attempt, and certainly never perform, any piece which cannot be properly accomplished. I only partly agree with whomever it was who said, 'If a thing is worth doing, it is worth doing badly.' Attempt it badly in private by all means but never inflict an unworthy performance on others; performances by the Portsmouth Symphonia were, after all, intended as a joke!

Choir work has brought me into contact with some wonderful people and despite all the heartaches of running a choir, and there were many, I wouldn't have missed it for the world. Singing side by side with French, German and Dutch friends, where music is the common language, has been a most rewarding experience and sharing their homes, albeit for very short periods, has highlighted that there are so many concerns, joys and sadnesses common to ordinary people from all nations, and for a short span of time the world becomes a much smaller place.

Sine Nomine, who gained first place with very high marks in the Cromer Festival in 1981 certainly contributed to the musical life in Norwich and Norfolk, performing in special services in the Cathedral and many other churches, at garden parties and a variety of other locations, in support of fund-raising events. One of the most popular items in these concerts was my setting of *Four Northumbrian Folksongs* which were taken up by numerous choirs and featured in the National Association of Choirs Choral Spectacular in Newcastle-upon-Tyne City Hall in 2001.

My work with Sine Nomine was very much a partnership with Isabel. In its earliest days we had practised in Isabel's home but then as membership increased we used the hall of the Jessopp Road United Reformed Church. Isabel acted as librarian and in so doing brought her considerable experience of singing in choirs to bear on the choice of repertoire and programme content.

With her crystal clear soprano voice she had sung as a student in the Chorus of the London University Music Society under John Russell, then the Cambridge University Music Society Chorus under Sir David Willcocks with whom she took part in a recording of Britten's *Voices for Today*. In a concert in Ely Cathedral she had sung under the direction of Britten himself and under Imogen Holst in Gustav Holst's *Hymn of Jesus*. In Detroit she sang with the chorus of the Detroit Symphony in Bloch's *Sacred Service*, sung in Hebrew, and Mahler's Second Symphony, (Resurrection), just after the assassination of Martin Luther King. On her return to England she joined the University of East Anglia Choir at first under Philip Ledger and subsequently under Peter Aston then the Aldeburgh Festival Singers which were drawn in part from the UEA choir.

Isabel went to Kettering High School for Girls where her English mistress was a Russian emigrée named Miss Marina Sharf. Isabel discovered later that Miss Scharf had become a Russian Orthodox Abbess, Mother Thekla, and lived in The Monastery of the Assumption just south of Whitby in North Yorkshire. As Miss Sharf she had been such an inspiring teacher, particularly of Shakespeare, and as Mother Thekla she had become the composer John Tavener's librettist. Isabel felt that we should try to meet up with her and following an exchange of letters, a visit was arranged and so we set off for, and managed to find, the monastery, a minimal establishment where Mother Thekla lived in the most Spartan of conditions. There also lived on the same site Father

Ephraim who was, by the purest coincidence, to be part of a significant event in Norwich Cathedral. In 1989 Michael Nicholas, was staging one of his Contemporary Church Music Festivals at Norwich Cathedral where he was Organist and Master of the Choristers. As part of the festival, Michael Nicholas arranged to perform John Taverner's *All-night Vigil* service and the composer would attend. Isabel was part of the choir assembled for this event and they set about learning the piece. Michael had decided to enlist the help of Father Ephraim, who was to be the celebrant, with a view to achieving a performance as authentic in style as possible. Michael wished to contact Fr Ephraim and when he learned that we were to visit the monastery where he was, entrusted Isabel with a message for him, which, on our visit to Mother Thekla was duly passed on. Father Ephraim subsequently attended a rehearsal in Norwich Cathedral and as the said rehearsal was in progress the distinctive figure of this Russian Orthodox priest with his stove pipe hat and lengthy beard arrived between the choir stalls and was introduced to the singers. 'And of course, you already know Isabel Watson,' said Michael to the great astonishment of them all.

Early on in our acquaintance Isabel had decided to further her own musical development as a solo singer. To that end she asked me to help her prepare for Associated Board examinations by gaining her Grade V Theory examination, the gateway to the more advanced practical examinations. This she achieved with consummate ease and thereafter I found myself as accompanist in her subsequent singing examinations. We steadily built up a repertoire of songs which we felt we could perform in public and so we did make ourselves available for singing in concerts and recitals. It was no mean repertoire including as it did 'The Sally Gardens' by Britten, 'Mandoline' by Fauré, 'Sure on this Shining Night' by Barber and many other staple pieces in the song repertoire by Schumann, Brahms and Bach and arias by Haydn and Handel.

In 1986, both being free from our first marriages, we decided that our futures lay together and we tied the knot in December of that year. As part of the Blessing Service, Sine Nomine sang a setting by me of Psalm 67, the hymn 'Lord, we come to ask your blessing' specially written for us by Fred Pratt Green was sung, and we marched out of the church to the *Toccatina* from my *St Wilfrid Suite* played by David Morgan. Since then Isabel has been an essential part of my musical development and as a discerning musician she would often pass comment on pieces I was composing, making suggestions which were invariably heeded.

In addition to its reciprocal arrangements with the Dutch, French and German choirs, Sine Nomine helped to accommodate two other choirs from further afield. In 1989 there appeared in the *Church Music Quarterly* a notice seeking English choirs to host the choir of the University of Lublin for a two-week tour of England. They would arrive with minimal resources, $US200 between forty of them. Aided financially by the local Polish Society, we picked them up by coach from Heathrow Airport and brought them to Norwich where they were lodged with local families. Under the direction of their conductor, Ursula Bobryk, they performed in St John's RC Cathedral, Norwich and Ely Cathedrals. The plan was that after five days they would move on to their next venues in Northampton and Crowthorne in Berkshire. Unfortunately the middle part of the arrangement fell through and they were not able to proceed to the third venue until the date original fixed. We were faced with accommodating them for a further five days in Norwich. This situation set in train an extraordinary outpouring of generosity from the people and businesses of Norwich who offered accommodation and hospitality in response to a notice in the local press. A meeting was held in our house to set up the continued arrangements at which their official chaperone, Professor Popov, presented us with a (still wet!) watercolour of a vase of flowers in the house where he was staying, which he had produced with

with the paints and paper he had with him. We promised him that we would have it framed and we were able to do this before the group left. We held up his framed picture for him to see as their coach finally left.

Another city twinned with Norwich is Novi Sad in Serbia (part of the former Yugoslavia) and in 1999 the choir of St George's Cathedral in that city came to Norwich and performed in Norwich Cathedral. Once again the members of Sine Nomine acted as hosts and Isabel and I put up their director Bogdan Djakovic and his fiancée. I set to and wrote them a setting of 'Gracious Spirit Holy Ghost' for their forthcoming wedding. The choir paid a return visit to Norwich in 2002 and included this anthem in their Norfolk & Norwich Festival concert programme in Norwich Cathedral. During that concert I was seated a long way from the platform on which they were performing at the west end of the cathedral. After my piece Bogdan gestured from the podium for me to go forward and join him on the platform. I started to make my way forward, picking my way through the densely packed audience and was taking such a long time. By the time I was within reach of the platform Bogdan had concluded that I was not coming forward and proceeded with the rest of the programme. I then had to pick my way back to where I had come from. The anthem was eventually sung at Bogdan's wedding, albeit to a different young lady from the one he had brought with him to our home! Some weeks after the event I received a video recording of the choir singing it at the wedding, and some years later a professional CD on which it was included. The anthem has also found its way into the repertoire of Oriana, a very accomplished 'ensemble vocal' based in Rouen, formed from selected members of the Chorale Voix Unies by Gérard Carreau and directed by him.

As for music at City College, whilst Dr Croft was Principal there had been a great deal of music, not just concerts of classical music but also productions of musicals and operettas which involved staff and students alike in acting, orchestral playing, scene painting, make-up and the printing of programmes. There were productions of *My Fair Lady*, *La Belle Hélène*, *The Gondoliers* and *The Mikado* in some of which I took part. Dr Croft's successor was Dr Jack Lewis and it was whilst he was at the helm that life at the college began to dehumanise, a process which continued during the time of Caroline Neville. The Carol Service was moved from the Cathedral to St Peter Mancroft and then to St Alban's Church just behind the College. St Alban's Church, with its concrete roof, was a very cold place, particularly in the winter months but it was a wonderful place for music, having brilliant acoustics. David Morgan's brass ensemble sounded particularly exciting in there. Attendance at the Carol Service became very depleted when it was decided that it should take place in the evening and not during teaching hours on the last Friday of term as students scattered home to all parts of Norfolk. It was predictable that very soon after that it would be discontinued. The requirement for music and drama staff to include all extra-curricular activity on their timetables led to the discontinuation of the musical productions which staff and students used to do in their spare time out of goodwill. Over the next few years the goodwill of staff was eroded and class contact hours increased and every aspect of life at City College which had made it an enjoyable place to work disappeared. No more children's Christmas parties, no more sports tournaments preceding the summer holiday, no more anything which wasn't part of the diploma production line. We had had the best of it.

Publication at last

In my early days I was composing and arranging and sending off
scores to publishers with no success. Convinced I was not a duffer
as a composer I decided to take advice and some lessons. There
was, living at Salhouse, near Norwich a very prestigious music
publisher, William Elkin. I wrote to him and asked him to look
at some of my manuscripts and give me some clues as to why
publishers might not want to publish them. Everything he told me
was absolutely spot-on. He touched on issues like the fact that I
was unknown, the durations and levels of difficulty of the pieces
and the matter of copyright of any words I might have set. He
also very kindly set me some criteria and promised that if I were
to write a piece which met his criteria he would publish it. I went
away and wrote a setting of 'All My Hope on God is Founded'
(words long since out of copyright) and, true to his word, he
published it under Braydeston Press. This was my first published
piece. Another thing he was very assertive about was that it was
the job of a publisher to give music away, and for 'publisher' one
could also read 'composer', which I took very much to heart and
have certainly acted upon over the years. I remember handing a
copy of the published 'All my hope...' to Dr Jackson in the York
organ loft; I am not aware that he ever used it. I also sent a copy
to Conrad Eden and was somewhat taken aback some days later
when it arrived back bearing several pencil marks indicating details

which CWE had thought could have been improved upon and a short note saying, 'I wish you had let me see this first!'

Another published composer whose guidance I sought was Professor Peter Aston who held the Chair of Music at the University of East Anglia. He too spoke encouragingly of my music and suggested I pay meticulous attention to the written scores, leaving nothing unclear. Further guidance was sought from another established composer, Arthur Wills. I would go to his abode in The Almonry at Ely armed with scores and heed his observations on them. The prevailing message was that I was on the right track. One piece of advice he gave me, which I certainly took on board, was to make my music rhythmically interesting. 'Go away and listen to Bartok,' he advised. These outings to Ely invariably included me treating myself to lunch in the Old Fire Engine House which is certainly a cut above. 'I can't afford to eat there,' mused Arthur on one occasion, but then he probably didn't need to, being married to a superb cook in Mary, on the door of whose kitchen was a sign which read 'Genius at Work'.

The major breakthrough came for me, and I suspect for several other composers, in the shape of that controversial and enigmatic character, Barry Brunton. Early advertisements in musical journals declared that 'Christmas isn't Christmas without Oecumuse'. A new approach to music publishing had arrived. All Barry Brunton needed were the masters of any piece and he would run them off to order. Nothing ever went out of print. His earliest publications were in A5 format and looked quite amateurish – but they sold! He also published pieces which, whilst they were very good, did not get taken on by other publishers. Even established figures like Herbert Sumsion and John Sanders sent him music which he made available. It all went off to reviewers and was heralded in his *Superlist*. I first met Barry at his London premises in Bounds Green. I found him very affable, a firmly built young man with a boyish face, full of new ideas about the publishing of music.

'Oecumuse' was a very clever appellation for Barry Brunton's venture, suggesting as it did a combination of ecumenism and economy (œcumenism and œconomicus). Life in the Oecumuse camp was good but somewhat unconventional. I was uneasy about the salacious content of some of Barry Brunton's circular letters but chose to ignore them. I do know that they turned several would-be customers away from Oecumuse, which was not good for the composers. Indeed a totally inappropriate reference to one of London's finest lady organists and teachers as 'an antique grotesque' brought universal disapproval and certain compilations with risqué titles submitted to *Organists' Review* for review led to the editor of that magazine refusing to review anything from Oecumuse. This was terrible news for composers but fortunately matters were in due course resolved and the reviewing of Oecumuse publications resumed.

Barry's premises in Ely were designated *The Arthur Wills Ely Music Shop* in which, not surprisingly, publications by that eminent organist of Ely Cathedral were to the fore. He was meticulous in drawing up contracts, registering works with PRS and the like, obtaining permissions for references to other music in copyright, and getting music reviewed. He was somewhat devious, however, in the way he handled royalty payments and money generally. For any purchases made from Oecumuse, cheques had to be made payable to Barry Brunton, not Oecumuse. Payment of royalties came in various forms. One was by the inclusion of bank notes tucked in between pages of his circulated material. Another was by offsetting purchases against royalties earned, and a third was payment in kind. As Barry Brunton always had a stock of stationery, one could find oneself being paid in packets of A4 paper, computer ink cartridges or indeed any useful item of stationery. On one occasion I was paid in postage stamps. Another feature of Barry Brunton's business premises was that they were also where he lived, ate and slept.

My involvement with Barry Brunton was indubitably the launching pad for me as a published, performed and recorded composer. My *Toccata*, begun on Tees-side and completed in Norwich, was accepted by Oecumuse in 1980 and if you want to see what it looked like, then look no further than *The IAO Millennium Book* in which Kevin Bowyer sang its praises (he later recorded it at Holbrook School chapel). Inspection will reveal a range of techniques that were employed to produce the first score. There are some hand-drawn features, some typed words alongside Letraset notes, rests and such like. Then there began to emerge musicians who had sophisticated computer programmes capable of producing authentic-looking scores and for a couple of years before his demise, Barry Brunton would have some scores computer-set. Some of mine were produced by Loft Music.

Playing it myself from an A5 copy as the final voluntary in a service in a Norwich church, it caught the attention of the young David Trendell who included it in one of Norwich Cathedral's Bank Holiday recitals. That was its first performance in a recital and the first time that I had heard one of my own pieces performed. Not long afterwards I was enjoying the company of Donald Spinks, one of two Assistant Organists at Norwich Cathedral, at a dinner organised by the Norfolk Guild of Organists. We agreed to share a bottle of wine but when it came to settling up Donald found himself somewhat embarrassed because he hadn't enough cash on him to chip in for the wine. 'Never mind,' said I, giving him a copy of *Toccata*, 'play this at your next recital in the Cathedral and we'll call it quits' – and he did.

With my Fellowship of the Chartered Institute of Builders hat on, I was invited to their annual dinner which was to be held on 24th March 1990 in King's College, Cambridge and which was always preceded by an organ recital in the chapel. I wondered how many of my builder colleagues had composed any organ music (not very many I suspect). I found out who would be giving the recital and it turned out to be Anne Page, a gifted young Australian player. Somewhat tongue-in-cheek I sent her a copy of *Toccata* and she very kindly agreed to include it the programme; and a very fine performance of it it was too!

Winning the Hugh Longstaff Memorial Trophy at the North of England Musical Tournament in 1953 had been entirely the result of the initiative of my friend Michael Addison; it would never have occurred to me at that time to enter any competition, I am not fundamentally a competitive person. In later life I came to believe that pitting one's wits against dependable yardsticks in order to see how one measured up would be no bad thing. Success would mean affirmation that one was of the standard that one believed oneself to have reached.

In 1988 Isabel spotted that The Royal School of Church Music was launching the annual Harold Smart Memorial Competition to encourage the composition of simple anthems, with or without organ accompaniment, for performance within the context of a church service and designed for choirs of fairly modest attainment. A notice to this effect appeared in the *Church Music Quarterly* which we received by virtue of the fact that Sine Nomine was affiliated to the RSCM.

Some years earlier when on a visit to Amsterdam, I had been given a small book entitled *Olney Hymns*, by a Dutch gentleman who had found it in a jumble sale and felt he had no further use for it and offered it to me. What a good job he did! The book, published in 1868 by T Nelson & Sons, Edinburgh and New York measuring a mere 4" x 2" x ½" thick is actually four books in one. Most of the works are by William Cowper and John Newton. 'Book First' contains hymns on selected passages of scripture. 'Book Second' contains hymns on occasional subjects, seasons, ordinances, providences and creation, 'Book Third' contains hymns on the rise, progress, changes and comforts of the spiritual life.

After this there are three poems. The preface is by John Newton and is dated February 15th 1779.

From 'Book Third' I chose to set Newton's words 'Confirm the Hope thy word allows', designated to be used 'before a sermon'. The adjudicators, Harry Brammah and Peter Aston, declared my entry, 'Confirm the Hope thy word allows' – (An Olney Hymn) to be the clear winner. Apart from the obvious delight at being the winner, the cash prize of £100 and publication by the RSCM, I felt a somewhat smug satisfaction that I, a lecturer in construction management at Norwich City College, had beaten off such distinguished opposition as established professional musicians, Robert Ashfield and Alan Bullard. The published score quite properly bears the dedication to Isabel. The first performance of the piece on 1st July 1989 was as the communion motet at the sung Eucharist which formed part of the Festival of Contemporary Church Music, referred to in the previous chapter. Adrian Lucas, the then Assistant Organist, accompanied. Norwich City College was well represented that morning as the final voluntary was 'Dancing on Air' by David Morgan who was by this time Head of Music at the College.

It was Isabel again who spotted a notice inviting entries for an organ suite in a competition promoted by Leeds Borough Council. My entry, entitled rather prosaically Suite for Leeds, was duly sent off under the pseudonym (one of the requirements of entry) of P Batcoh. Earlier that year we had been in the USSR (indeed one of the movements was written on the beach in Yalta) and I thought I was being very cunning in using as a pseudonym my real name but written in the Cyrillic alphabet. (In conversation with Simon Lindley some years later it came to light that someone in the office in Leeds was a Russian speaker and spotted my name straight away.) In this instance I was awarded second prize which brought with it a cash prize of £250 and the promise of performance by Simon Lindley. After several enquiries as to when the performance

1) Left: *St John's Church. The oldest church in Middlesbrough.*

2) Below: *Conrad Eden at the console of Durham Cathedral c. 1965.*

3) Bottom: *Winning the Hugh Longstaff Memorial Trophy at the North of England Musical Tournament in Newcastle upon Tyne.*

4) *Above: Dr Francis Jackson c. 1965.*
5) *Right: Revd Dr Fred Pratt Green.*
6) *Below: St Giles Church, Norwich.*

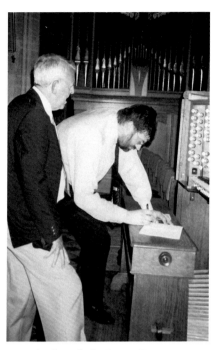

7) Above left: Kevin Bowyer autographs the author's programme after performing Rievaulx at St Mary's Standon.

8) Above right: With June Nixon at Lambeth Palace after her receiving her Lambeth Doctorate.

9) Below: Dr Gerald Gifford after performing Homage to Buxtehude on his own harpsichord at St Thomas's Church, Heigham, Norwich. L to r Brian Lincoln, the Very Rev'd Alan Warren, RW, and seated Gerald Gifford.

10) Top: Sine Nomine singing in the gardens of the Kloster Mariensee near Hanover.

11) Middle: With Gillian Ward Russell, Tim Patient, Dr Arthur Wills and David Dunnett at the author's seventieth birthday celebration in Norwich Cathedral.

12) Isabel.

would take place (I would have gone to hear it), I heard nothing and do not know whether or not he ever performed it. However, Francis Jackson, who had been one of the adjudicators and who was due to come to Norwich Cathedral to give a recital on the 3rd of August 1994, offered to include the piece, which he duly did and continued to perform it in recitals for some time to come. Within a week he performed it at St Martin-on-the-Hill, Scarborough and later at St Edmund's, Roundhay in Leeds, which we attended.

Another competition presented itself as part of the next Norwich Festival of Contemporary Church Music. It was for a setting of the evening canticles to be adjudicated by Peter Aston and Michael Nicholas. My setting included the use of clusters in the organ accompaniment and I was, and still am, quite proud of it. My entry did not win but wasn't consigned to oblivion as Michael Nicholas used it at one of the Cathedral Evensongs and it was taken up by Peter Moorse and his London Cantata Choir, and the St Cecilia Singers directed by Harrison (Fred) Oxley. Under their separate direction I heard the setting done in St Paul's Cathedral with Gary Seiling at the organ and in Peterborough Cathedral with John Jordan at the organ. It has also been used in Norwich Cathedral on a few occasions since. I remember sitting listening in a privileged position in the choir as St Paul's and thinking 'not bad for a quantity surveyor'!

On that theme, because the practice of music has always been a hobby and not my main source of income, I have frequently dwelt on the fact that some very fine music has been written and performed by amateur musicians whose first careers have been quite removed from music. Indeed wasn't Rimsky Korsakov a serving naval officer when he wrote his (and Russia's) first symphony?

The last competition I entered was for a Christmas carol promoted by the *Methodist Recorder* in 1991. A setting was being sought of words by Fred Pratt Green. I was at the time as close to Fred as anyone could get, his designated next of kin no less and collaborator in hymn and hymn tune writing. I asked him straight how he felt about me entering the competition and he thought I should, but of course without any of his involvement in any way. Entries were anonymous. I did in fact win the competition with 'One of the Children of the Year', received a cash prize of £75 and publication by Stainer & Bell. Since then I have not entered any competitions as I no longer feel that I have anything to prove.

In 2004 Barry Brunton disappeared, his car was found abandoned at Norwich railway station. His final base was in premises at Downham Market in Norfolk, which he leased from Adrian Flux at East Winch, about halfway between my home and Downham Market. Flux had cleared everything from the premises rented by Barry Brunton and had it all in terrapin buildings at the rear of his main premises. I was given the opportunity to go and sift through everything, my main interest being to retrieve the masters of my published compositions. Arthur Wills joined me on one visit and retrieved what he could find of his own works. As well as reclaiming my own masters, I collected others and let the composers know I had them. Some weeks later I found myself sending off cardboard boxes full of scores to the family of Herbert Sumsion and the widow of John Sanders amongst others.

Happily, the demise of Oecumuse coincided with the decision of Chris Duarte to venture into the world of publishing as Escorial Edition. Chris, at the time a lay clerk in Norwich Cathedral Choir, ran St George's Music Shop in Norwich for discerning musicians with his wife Anne (also an organist). When I learned of the emergence of Escorial Edition I approached Chris with three of my organ pieces and a choral piece which he accepted.

Soon after this in 2004 Geoffrey Atkinson, a composer formerly published by Barry Brunton, decided to go it alone with *fagus-music. com* and agreed to take over all my Oecumuse publications and accept me as one of his house composers. This has become the main source of my published music.

A widening audience

If publishing anything I wrote wasn't enough, Barry Brunton had asked June Nixon, the remarkable and celebrated Organist of St Paul's Cathedral Melbourne, if she might be interested in recording some of my output and he sent her a selection of scores. Happily she too was all for it and a sponsor was found and the recordings were duly made. June, with her husband Neville Finney, often visited the UK, usually en route to further afield and it was arranged that they should come and meet me at Norwich City College and then proceed to our home in Mattishall for an evening meal. We learned in conversation that they had both lived in Norwich some years earlier and it further transpired that June and I had passed like ships in the night, totally unaware of each other's existence, at an organ recital in Norwich Cathedral by Herrick Bunney. June had with her a cassette with one of the tracks of the CD she had already recorded and so as soon as we were indoors I played the track, *Prelude, Fugue and Carillon on Gopsal*. I was thrilled. This was the first time I had heard a recording of anything of my own and the playing was brilliant. Later that year the CD appeared and received excellent reviews, one of which cited my music as being the ideal vehicle for showing off the magnificent T C Lewis organ in Melbourne Cathedral. June named the ensuing CD *Jubiläum* after the piece with which the programme opens. A lasting friendship had been struck which would endure so in 2000 when June received her Lambeth Doctorate from Archbishop George Carey we were privileged to be present at the ceremony. On another occasion when we were together in 2013 it came to light that June, who had made the journey all the way from Australia, and I, who had made the journey all the way from Tees-side, took our ARCO examination on the same day and had played the same pieces. 'How spooky is that, possums?' as Dame Edna would say.

In 2001 when Isabel and I made our trip around the world, we stayed for several days with June and Neville and I gave a lunchtime recital in Melbourne Cathedral.

Once when on a holiday with my young family in Marbella in Spain I wandered into the beautiful church there and noticed a recital programme pinned on a notice board at the rear of the church. For some reason the name of the recitalist, Pilar Cabrera, stuck. Her programme, which included Franck's third *Choral*, left me in no doubt that this lady could play. It was some years later that I saw a feature in *Organist's Review* about this, very young and attractive, as it turned out, lady who was trying to arrange a recital tour of the UK. There were contact details and, heeding Bill Elkin's advice, I sent some of my scores off to Señora Cabrera with a covering letter which I had had translated into impeccable Spanish by one of the language lecturers at the City College. Surprisingly quickly, I had an enthusiastic reply and assurance that Pilar would be performing my music when a suitable opportunity presented itself. She was not only as good as her word but sent me a recording of her recital in Auditorio Alfredo Kraus in Las Palmas in which she had included a movement from *Suite for Leeds* and *Dances*.

I was thrilled to hear that she would be including *Jubiläum* in a recital in St Saviour's Cathedral, Bruges (Brugge) on 14th August 2003 and Isabel and I decided to go to hear her and to meet her. The recital was to be part of the cathedral's celebration of the organ's fiftieth birthday, or as it said on the posters 'JUBILEUMTIJD'.

How totally appropriate to include my piece written to mark the fiftieth anniversary of the Norfolk Organists' Association and what a touch of serendipity that I should have chosen that particular title for the piece! We travelled by Eurostar to Brussels, thence by train to Bruges. We made our way to our hotel, which turned out to be charming and homely. Its one drawback was its proximity to one of Bruges's waterways and we found ourselves sharing our bedroom with mosquitoes. We either had fresh air and mosquitoes or an airless and stuffy room without them. However, having settled into our own hotel, we wandered round to the hotel where Pilar was staying with her husband Michael Reckling and announced our presence. It was a great delight to meet them and as we were intending to go into the main square to find somewhere for an evening meal we suggested that they join us. The Spanish habitually eat very late indeed by our standards and they initially thought that eating at about 7 pm was far too early for them but decided to join us anyway in order that we could converse and get to know each other.

It came to light that even her appearance in Bruges was at one point in some doubt as prior to leaving she had been feeling not at all well, but she had decided to go ahead with it after all. I spent some time with her on the day of the recital preparing *Jubiläum* during which time we met Ignace Michiels, Organist at the Cathedral, who invited Isabel and me back with Pilar and Michael for a meal after the recital along with an Italian organist, who was scheduled to give the next recital, and his wife. Conversation flowed in a variety of languages that evening!

Pilar's recital was a triumph and the experience was crowned by her producing out of the blue a copy of *Badinage* which I had sent her, and playing it as an encore. Ignace was so taken with the piece that he asked for a copy. At my suggestion Pilar gave him her copy there and then and I sent her a replacement when I got home. I also sent her the score of *Pastorale* which I had written for her.

I was further thrilled to discover some months later that Ignace had included *Badinage* on a CD from St Saviour's Cathedral which came out in 2005. It is amazing how one thing leads to another.

We would be in the company of Pilar and Michael again in 2004. They had in the meantime moved from Marbella to a small village in Castile and Leon, Cubillas de Santa Marta, where Michael had been instrumental in getting an Allen Custom Renaissance three manual organ installed in the thirteenth-century church and the village were very proud of this indeed. We had been delighted to learn that on 21st June that year Pilar had given birth to Lorenzo. Whilst in Bruges they had confided in us the difficulties they were having starting a family and so the news that they finally had a son filled us with particular pleasure. I wrote an organ piece for the newborn which I entitled *Cradle Song* which appears as part of *Mrs Thing's Christmas Stocking* but Geoffrey Atkinson kindly agreed to print a single copy which I could send to Pilar. They had also planned a recital in the church for the last weekend in October which would be part of the village's celebrations of the wine harvest. In addition during that same weekend Lorenzo was to be baptised. Isabel and I were invited and I would play some items in the recital and during the baptism would play *Cradle Song*. They undertook to look after all our accommodation and eating needs during our stay; it all sounded as though it would be a lovely few days. The reality, sadly, didn't quite match our expectations. We are entirely content with 'modest' when it comes to subsistence but we were quite taken aback by the provisions which had been made for us.

We flew into Valladolid airport where it had been arranged that Michael would meet us. Entering the Arrivals hall we were somewhat alarmed to discover that Michael was not there. Quite quickly the other passengers were met and whisked away leaving us the last people remaining in the seemingly deserted terminal building. We explored ideas of how we could contact anyone but came up with none. Not before time Michael did swing into the car park to our considerable relief and took us to our accommodation. It looked like an old fort and the problem was that the proprietor seemed not to be expecting us, but when pressed by Michael led us into what would be our sleeping accommodation, a small, barely-decorated cell of a room with two camp beds about a yard apart between which was one chair, the only provision for storing our clothes. And it was cold, so cold that we enquired about heating and were within a few minutes given a small one-bar electric fire which was totally ineffective. We were quite disconsolate. Having settled in, for want of a better expression, we were then driven to meet Pilar at their new premises. They had bought a derelict property which they intended to refurbish whilst living on the site in a mobile home. We were also shown the church and organ.

We passed a very cold night and were presented with a minimal breakfast which included a pastry each, the wrappers of which indicated that they were months past their sell-by date. To the side of the breakfast area was a bar counter at which men sat drinking, seeming totally unfazed by the explicit sexual activity on the television screen behind the counter that seemed to be permanently tuned to the Spanish adult channel. We had no transport, for if we had we would certainly have found better accommodation in Valladolid and footed the bill ourselves. We were entirely dependent on Michael for getting about and for taking us for our pre-arranged meals in a transport café where we ate alone and were collected afterwards. It was all quite soul-destroying. On the day of the concert we were left at the church for me to practise but left there a very long time. The wait was relieved to some extent by a wedding which took place in the church. It was interesting to observe, which we did from the rear of the church to the side of the organ. We were particularly taken by the women looking most elegant in their mantillas. We were, for all that, still cold and hungry. When we were eventually collected it was feared that Pilar, who was not feeling at all well, might have to pull out of the recital and serious consideration was given to me doing the whole recital on my own. We drove to a nearby clinic into which Pilar went for an assessment of her condition from which she emerged having decided to go ahead.

The concert was a great success with the church virtually filled to capacity and afterwards we all went to the wine tasting where there were local cheeses and nibbles of which we surreptitiously took rather more than would normally be expected. Very much later, Pilar's closer entourage went to a small restaurant in the village where, somewhere approaching midnight we had the chance of some real food. It was a warm and friendly gathering and there was much conversation about music. We were given a lift back to our accommodation by a kind Spanish gentleman by the name of Jesus (there are a lot of them about), who gave us a very hairy ride. And so, again, to two very cold beds.

The day of Lorenzo's baptism was a revelation. After the ceremony all the guests returned to the Old Fort where we were staying and to which we would see a different side. A long table was set out in a splendid room and several courses of the most exquisite food were served and we enjoyed the company of Pilar's family and close friends. In fairness I think Pilar and Michael had rather a lot on their plates at that time in their lives, living with a new-born baby in makeshift accommodation, and in offering to look after us during our visit had bitten off a little more than they could chew. Michael took us to the airport the next day and we parted on optimistic terms. Pilar is now Organist at Valladolid Cathedral and appears to be putting that place on the musical map.

Euterpe & Co

The Greeks attributed artistic inspiration to The Muses; no doubt and before very long, neurologists will be able to explain quite scientifically how 'inspiration' arises.

In my own case I think musical ideas either came into being of their own accord (Euterpe at work), or were triggered in some other way. Those that simply came into my consciousness seemingly from nowhere I think of as ear-worms, little tunes and rhythms which suddenly one is aware of going round and round in one's head. If such an idea has real potential then no time can be lost in capturing it, which for me invariably meant grabbing the nearest scrap of paper, hastily drawing five parallel lines and jotting down the notes and basic rhythm.

Several of my published compositions started life as ear-worms; certainly *Toccata* which was born in Thornaby-on-Tees, *Minuet à Trois* which was scribbled on a sheet of headed notepaper in a hotel in Yalta, amongst others. Having settled on the opening bars of a piece one is faced with the question 'where do I go from here?' and the process of composition begins. Ideas follow ideas and sometimes lead up blind alleys but I am convinced that at any point in any composition there is only one legitimate way for the music to proceed and often this is a case of trial and error, witness the crossings out that can be found in the manuscripts of even the great masters. It is immensely frustrating to have an idea that enables the music to move and then be unable to recapture it and write it down. I have every sympathy with the poor soul 'seated one day at the organ' who stumbled across the perfect chord (The Lost Chord), and subsequently could never rediscover it.

When there isn't an ear-worm then there have to be other reasons for embarking on a composition. A large proportion of my output is the result of of suggestions and requests, 'Why don't you write something for manuals only?'; 'Can you write me a piece based on *Urbs Beata?*'; 'Will you write me something in memory of my late wife? Her favourite piece was...'

Having had such an approach the problem is where to start. The latter two are relatively easy with the existing tunes involved giving something to build on. 'Something for manuals only' is more of a problem. In the absence of any ear-worms my approach would be simply to sit at the keyboard and doodle in the hope that sooner or later something might come out of the ends of my fingers which could be turned into a viable piece. I am sure that a great many composers have done this. I once heard it said that much of Chopin's finest music simply went out of the window.

Requests and suggestions for pieces came thick and fast from Oecumuse. At Barry Brunton's behest I produced *Three Handel Hymn Tune Preludes* to mark the 300th anniversary of the composer's birth and *Elegy in Memoriam Herbert Howells* which found me sitting at my home organ with my left foot on B. Why B? Because in German notation, B natural is H and how better to start a piece dedicated to Herbert Howells than with two consecutive Bs in the pedal? For the 'what next' stage I simply did what most organists frequently have to do during services to maintain continuity, extemporise. This I did with Howells's well known hymn tune *Michael* in mind. Extemporisation often throws up ideas which are worth pursuing and the piece soon started to take shape. Reference to *Michael* was incorporated (with the permission of its owners) with the piece reaching a peaceful conclusion in the same way as it began, with HH in the pedal.

I dedicated *Introduction Passacaglia & Fugue* (an ear-worm) to a gifted local organist Bryan Ellum who subsequently became a great champion of my music, suggesting and requesting pieces and performing them. The same piece caught the attention of Michael Fleming who, on one occasion played it at Walsingham where we went to listen. Michael Fleming was a reviewer of choral and organ music for CMQ and always wrote glowingly about my output. Bryan commissioned a piece from me for his partner, Jane Berry which bore the title *Dances* (an ear-worm), which was jotted down on a train somewhere between York and Peterborough, and she gave that its first performance in Princes Street URC in Norwich. Jane and Bryan were close friends of the distinguished organist and harpsichordist Gerald Gifford and commissioned a harpsichord piece from me for him. It is entitled *Homage to Buxtehude* and features Gerald's initials in Morse Code in the final section. He performed this several times in my presence, on one occasion in a concert in St Thomas's Church, Heigham alongside pieces by two other composers, Brian Lincoln and The Very Rev'd Alan Warren. *Jubiläum* had been composed at the suggestion of Francis Jackson who had been invited to give a recital in Norwich Cathedral to mark the fiftieth anniversary of the Norfolk Organists' Association in 1997. On that occasion Dr Jackson used the piece to both open and conclude the recital, hence it really had world premières. (But only just; less than twenty-four hours later June Nixon would play it as the final voluntary at a Choral Eucharist in St Paul's Cathedral, Melbourne.) The newly arrived David Dunnett turned the pages. Dr Jackson also gave the piece several airings and included it in a recital at York Minster which was recorded.

In her capacity as the Regional Liaison Officer of the Incorporated Association of Organists for the East of England, Dr Gillian Ward Russell attended those same celebrations and expressed an interest in *Jubiläum* and I made sure she received a copy. Gillian played the piece in a recital in St Paul's Cathedral on 30th April 2000 which I was unable to attend as I was in Rouen with Sine Nomine. On the actual day of the recital we were singing in Caudebec-en-Caux. As soon as her recital was over, Gillian wrote me a very detailed letter about the recital and her registration of the piece. Happily Gillian became a great champion of my music, commissioning and playing my pieces in Maldon and various other locations, even at the Edinburgh Festival. For her I wrote *Excursion* and *Maldon Suite* (which she played in Germany), having given both their first performances in Maldon. The suite involved quite a bit of research into facets of life in Maldon including a local giant who is depicted in one of the movements. Through her good offices I was commissioned to write a piece for the Diamond Jubilee of the Chelmsford and District Organists' Association. The result of this was *Festivo*, premièred by Gillian in Chelmsford Cathedral on 4th June 2010.

June Nixon and her husband Neville Finney visited us in the January of 1998 and we invited David Dunnett and his wife Nicky to join us for an evening meal. On that occasion David indicated that if I were to write a piece for him he would play it in his summer recital. So I wrote *Concert Piece* which exploits David's considerable virtuosity (there are one or two tight corners), which he duly played as promised and which was later recorded by Paul Derrett as part of his Benchmarks series of CDs on the organ of The Church of St Peter & St Paul, Wisbech. Since that time David Dunnett has been a regular performer of my pieces both locally and abroad (even Russia) and has recorded my *Sonatina* on CD and 'Kum ba 'yah' on DVD. I owe him a great debt of gratitude.

The aforementioned Ralph Bootman had a birthday which coincided with an event at Oxnead Mill organised by the NGO. There was at this old mill building a collection of organs which members could enjoy playing. Only a few hours before setting off for the evening's festivities I penned a spoof chorale prelude on 'Happy Birthday' using Bach's Schübler Prelude *Wachet Auf* as the basis. I played it on one of the theatre organs as someone brought in a birthday cake, suitably illuminated. Barry Brunton, having obtained the necessary permissions (did you know that the copyright of 'Happy Birthday to You' is owned by two American ladies?) published the piece as 'Happy Birthday Herr Bach', which is now known worldwide.

As we drove in through the outskirts of Corby in Northamptonshire on one occasion to visit my wife's family, traffic was momentarily brought to a standstill as a funeral cortège made its way into a churchyard. At the head of the cortège was a piper in full highland dress. With nothing much on my mind as we sat and waited, I mused on the possibility of writing an organ piece based on a drone and in pentatonic mode. One of the most distinctive features of any piece of music performed on the bagpipes is the sound that emerges as the wind reservoir fills up with the individual reeds gradually and eventually speaking at their true pitch. This effect could be achieved on an organ, I thought, if the performance were to begin before the blower had been switched on and the bellows had filled up. To this end the player is directed to wedge down the two notes of the drone with stops drawn and then to switch on the organ's blower. Over this drone, music of a distinctively Scottish character is played and at the end, the blower switched off to allow the instrument to wheeze once more into silence. However, modern wind supply systems are more efficient than earlier ones and when June Nixon recorded this piece in Melbourne Cathedral she had to achieve these effects by other means.

On another occasion I was watching an act on television involving a troupe of Chinese acrobats who were performing with diabolos (stringless yo-yos) which they threw to each other from what looked like skipping ropes. There was a very distinctive and regular rhythm in their actions which conjured up in my mind the music which was to become *Badinage* which bounces along in a carefree way.

A noteworthy commission came from Kevin Bowyer who had the idea of placing in five English abbeys a CD containing pieces which depicted them. Being a Yorkshireman I chose *Rievaulx* and went to hear Kevin play it on two occasions, at St Mary's Standon in 2001 and St Giles Cripplegate in 2005. Kevin too has been a good champion of my music. It was at the recital in St Mary's Standon that I met up again with Martin Penny who was there with his wife. Martin's musical career had flourished and he was at that time Organist at All Saints Hertford. At that meeting he asked me to write something for him, the result of which was *Four A Penny*, a four movement suite which Martin launched in a recital in Hertford in 2002 which we attended.

In the same way that Barry Brunton would suggest compositions, Geoffrey Atkinson has also fed me some ideas over the years. One of the most fruitful was a suggestion for pieces for beginners and what are often referred to as 'reluctant organists'; people who are competent pianists who find themselves pressed to play the organ for services. As Geoffrey put it, 'the sort of thing Mrs Thing from the village could play for voluntaries'. 'Why not a Suite for Mrs Thing?' I ventured. And so it was. The *Suite for Mrs Thing* definitely hit the mark and is widely used. The hint 'why not something for manuals only' prompted *Mrs Thing puts her feet up*. The printed scores of these are adorned on the front cover by amusing and imaginative illustrations by Martin Cottam.

In the same vein I produced *Mrs Thing's Christmas Stocking* and *Mrs Thing's Easter Egg*.

In 2000 our village of Mattishall held a village festival known as the Gant inspired by the old Rogationtide hiring fair, which was a major undertaking featuring pageants representing significant events in the village's history. One of these was the finding of a hoard of Roman coins. Villagers dressed up as Iceni and Romans and enacted the discovery of the hoard. I was invited to compose some incidental music that would be played over loudspeakers at the site of the discovery. One of the pieces was a fanfare and the brass ensemble at Dereham's Neatherd High School was engaged to come to a recording studio in the village and record it. There was a useful spin-off from the Gant as, not long afterwards, Bryan Ellum asked me for a suite for him to use in recitals. Well he didn't get a suite but what emerged was my *Sonatina* of which Bryan gave the first performance in Cromer Parish Church in June 1991. Rather than waste it, I used my Gant Fanfare for the opening of the *Sonatina*. Shortly after this Isabel and I went off to Canada and on our return were surprise and thrilled to learn that David Dunnett had recorded the piece in The English Cathedral Series.

In 2006, in order to raise funds for a tour of the USA by the choir of Norwich Cathedral, one of the fund-raising ideas was an auction of promises. My contribution was to offer to write either an organ or choral piece for the highest bidder with the guiding figure being £8 per minute of music. I was subsequently intrigued to learn that the highest bidder was Nicky Dunnett who requested a five-minute organ piece.

As the main congregation filed into the cathedral on Sunday mornings, Nicky could often be seen heading out of the Cathedral Close clutching a guitar. She is known to be very fond of the less formal style of worship and its music so I decided to write something for her based on a more popular worship song and 'Kum Ba 'yah' sprang to mind. Each short variation is based on a line in the hymn; 'someone's praying, Lord; someone's crying, Lord' and so on. Not surprisingly I had the Norwich Cathedral organ in mind when writing this piece and it is not difficult to be imaginative when writing for an instrument on which any combination of stops one might desire is possible. David included the piece for its first performance in his recital on 15th August 2007 and included it in the programme of music on the DVD of the Norwich Cathedral organ released in 2013. Geoffrey Atkinson always features an appropriate picture on the front of his published scores and I was delighted to be able to provide for this score a photograph I had taken on the shores of Lake Victoria of local Tanzanian people walking along the water's edge in their finest clothes on Christmas Day 2004.

There has been some financial remuneration from commissions but more often I have received payment in kind. Jane and Bryan invariably treated Isabel and me to some fine dining and from others there have been cases of wine and in one instance a carton of assorted French cheeses. Whilst happily accepting these initial rewards for my labours, further rewards in the form of sales, performances and recordings are equally enjoyable.

Words and music

The renowned Methodist hymn-writer Dr Fred Pratt Green moved to Norwich in retirement in 1968, coincidentally at about the same time I had. When I was Organist at St Giles, there appeared on the music desk of the organ some time in 1985 the words of a hymn typed on a flimsy piece of A5 paper on an old-fashioned typewriter. The title of the hymn, which was sung to the tune 'Herongate', was 'In Honour of St Giles' and was there because the then Vicar at St Giles, Canon Frank Millett, had asked Fred Pratt Green for a hymn in honour of that saint. I had recently written a hymn tune with somewhat quirky rhythms which I thought might make an interesting carol. Discovering that Fred Pratt Green lived only a few miles away in Thorpe St Andrew, I decided to send the tune to him and ask if he might consider writing words for it.

As a result I received a phone call from Fred who suggested that I should go to see him the following Friday morning and that phone call changed both of our lives. I took myself, armed with my tune, to his pleasant semi-detached house in Hillcrest Road in Thorpe St Andrew, Norwich, where Fred lived with his wife Marjorie, herself an acknowledged preacher. He admitted having had difficulty getting the hang of my tune and nothing further came of it. However, we hit it off immediately and from then on I met Fred for a half-day every week until his death in 2000. We played hymn tunes, co-composed hymns, talked about anything and everything and in the process produced the material which would become the follow-on to the book *The Hymns and Ballads of Fred Pratt Green*, entitled *Later Hymns and Ballads and Fifty Poems* both of which are published by Stainer & Bell in this country and The Hope Publishing Company in the United States. I was often present when Fred would receive a print-out of his royalty earnings from Hope. They were printed on one continuous sheet of computer paper and when held up would be longer than the man himself! The sums involved were also substantial. Fred knew he could never be comfortable amassing such sums from his hymn-writing and set up The Pratt Green Trust which would fund projects related to hymnody, notably the online Hymnquest database. At the time of his death his personal possessions were very few. I once asked him if he had ever considered writing his own memoirs. He had, but had ruled it out on the grounds that he could never tell the whole truth. There were things in his life which it would not benefit anyone to know and there are probably still those to the fore who would be hurt by their disclosure.

On one memorable evening he and the Rt Rev'd Timothy Dudley Smith, Bishop of Thetford and himself a prolific hymn writer, compared their approaches to writing hymns. One startling fact emerged. The Bishop admitted that he was totally tone-deaf and had no idea what tunes his hymns were sung to. Fred, on the other hand, often wrote hymns with particular tunes in mind and when we were writing hymns together he was very particular about which tunes fitted his words.

Fred and Marjorie had no children but Fred had a nephew and nieces, none of whom was near at hand. They had been guardians, in the absence of her missionary parents, to the actress Elizabeth Shepherd, whom they regarded as a daughter, and she lived partly in Canada and the United States. On one occasion when Fred and Marjorie had obviously been discussing their future, being both in their eighties, Fred asked me if I would act as his next of kin, a request to which I readily agreed. They took a difficult decision, when they realised that continuing to live where they were was increasingly difficult, to move into the Methodist Home for the Aged, Cromwell House, in Cecil Road in Norwich. In Cromwell House they had single rooms next door to each other and they ate in the dining room with the other residents. Fred was very happy there as he was used to and liked communal living. Marjorie was less happy though acknowledged that it was the best place for them at their age. This was less than a five-minute walk from Norwich City College where I worked which meant that keeping a watchful eye on them as they became increasingly frail was very easy.

My association with Fred led unexpectedly to a reunion with Dr Francis Jackson. In 1957 Francis Jackson had written the hymn tune *East Acklam* for the hymn 'God that Madest Earth and Heaven' as an alternative to the Welsh tune *Ar Hyd y Nos* (All through the night). *East Acklam*, named after the village near Malton in North Yorkshire where Francis Jackson had bought the cottage in which he now lives, was first used to this hymn at the 1957 Old Choristers' Re-union and then at the York Diocesan Choir Festival in which my choir from St John's, Middlesbrough took part. How Dr Jackson's tune came to be wedded to Fred Pratt Green's 'Harvest Hymn' is well documented in Dr Jackson's autobiography *Music for a Long While*. Incredibly the two men must have passed like ships in the night when Fred was Chairman of the York and Hull Methodist District between 1957 and 1964 and was often in York and occasionally in the Minster. At an IAO conference at Durham in 1992 I met Dr Jackson for the first time since my move to Norwich in 1968. At that meeting, Dr Jackson asked, amongst other things, if I knew Fred Pratt Green, indicating how much he would like to meet him. When I explained that I knew Fred very well indeed, being his acting next of kin, it was proposed that as Dr Jackson was coming to Norwich to accompany a visiting choir in Norwich Cathedral, we would arrange for the two men to meet.

At my next meeting with Fred I told him of the proposed arrangement to meet Francis Jackson and he was very thrilled indeed at the prospect; he considered *East Acklam* the best modern hymn tune he had encountered. Marjorie at that time was in her terminal illness and was receiving exemplary care at Cromwell House. Isabel and I had arranged an evening meal which was to include Francis and Priscilla Jackson and Fred and Marjorie but it was clear that as Marjorie was now bed-fast, Fred would come on his own. The Jacksons also had with them Priscilla's sister-in-law who lived at Stradsett in Norfolk and who had attended Evensong. Isabel picked Fred up from Cromwell House and took him to the Cathedral and after the service, when everyone had met up, they all came back to our cottage in Mattishall for dinner. Over that evening meal both men autographed the hymn in my copy of *Hymns for Today's Church*. This must be something of a rarity! Whilst he controlled it very well, Fred was noticeably anxious to get back to Cromwell House and Marjorie as soon as was politely possible.

After Marjorie had died Fred and Francis would meet a couple of times more. On a subsequent occasion when Dr Jackson was staying with us, we went together to visit him in Cromwell House. Dr Jackson had with him the score of his setting of Fred's words 'When in our music God is glorified' which he had written for Dennis Townhill's birthday and wanted Fred to autograph it. On our arrival at Cromwell House, Fred was asleep in an armchair in the main entrance hall but didn't mind being woken up; he often just nodded off at the drop of a hat. Despite a very shaky hand, Fred appended his signature to the manuscript and that would be the last time the two men met.

Fred Pratt Green died in 2000 aged ninety-seven and his funeral was held in Chapelfield Methodist Church in Norwich for which I played and in response to a request from Bernard Braley, Fred's publisher and executor, I improvised for a few minutes on the tune *East Acklam* as Fred had declared it to be his favourite modern hymn tune. The improvisation was later to be published by Escorial Edition as *Meditation on East Acklam*. The following year at a Memorial Service for Fred in Wesley's Chapel in City Road in London, Dr Jackson and I shared the playing, in that Dr Jackson played voluntaries before and after the service and I accompanied the hymns, except 'For the fruits of his creation', which was accompanied by the composer. Included in the pre-service music were Dr Jackson's own *Prelude on East Acklam* and my *Meditation*.

We had several outings with Fred and Marjorie, one in particular sticks in the memory. Fred's American publisher, Hope Publishing of Carol Stream, Illinois, held a centenary dinner in the Liberal Club in London for their London-based contacts and associates. The four of us were invited and were given accommodation in an adjacent hotel. On our arrival in the hotel's reception we asked the receptionist to let George Shorney, the Managing Director of Hope Publishing know that we had arrived. 'Mr Shorney is coming straight down,' she told us. Within a very short time the doors of the lift opened and out strode the tall and elegant Mr Shorney. He greeted us all very warmly; 'Hi Raarn, hi Isabel,' he said, shaking us enthusiastically by the hand as though we were a long-lost brother and sister. Having got to our rooms, we spruced ourselves up for the dinner, and when the time came we made our way to the dining room to be greeted as we entered by George Shorney and his wife with the words, 'And you are?'

My years with Fred were marvellous – an experience to be cherished and one which could never be repeated. When Isabel and I married in December 1986 we sang a hymn written for the occasion by Fred, 'Lord we come to ask your blessing', which is included in *Later Hymns and Ballads and Fifty Poems*. Wherever I am in the world I usually look in the local hymn book and invariably find at least one of Fred's hymns, often more than one, and realise what a major hymn writer he was.

286

EAST ACKLAM 8 4 8 4 8 8 8 4

© Francis Jackson (born 1917)

1 For the fruits of his creation,
  thanks be to God;
  for his gifts to every nation,
  thanks be to God;
  for the ploughing, sowing, reaping,
  silent growth while we are sleeping,
  future needs in earth's safe-keeping,
  thanks be to God.

2 In the just reward of labour,
  God's will is done;
  in the help we give our neighbour,
  God's will is done;
  in our worldwide task of caring
  for the hungry and despairing,
  in the harvests we are sharing,
  God's will is done.

3 For the harvests of his Spirit,
  thanks be to God;
  for the good we all inherit,
  thanks be to God;
  for the wonders that astound us,
  for the truths that still confound us,
  most of all, that love has found us,
  thanks be to God.

F. Pratt Green (born 1903)
© Stainer & Bell Ltd

F.Rutherford.
Francis Jackson
15 May 1993
Norwich.

A significant association with Durham also exists as the University of Durham houses The Pratt Green Hymnology Collection which was formally opened on 15th October 1987.

In the congregation at St Giles were Peter and Noreen Pope with whom Isabel and I became very friendly. They were both fine musicians. Noreen had many piano pupils and Peter, also a fine pianist, composed. He had been a pupil of Cyril Smith and had studied composition with John Ireland and, more remarkably, with Nadia Boulanger. At one stage Augener offered to publish anything and everything that he wrote. However, when he met Noreen she belonged a religious sect, The Raven-Taylor Bretheren, which banned involvement with the arts. Despite this, Peter married Noreen and to the considerable dismay of his friends, he set music aside and did not resume composing until 1971.

Isabel and I spent many happy hours with the Popes, not a few of them involving eating; Peter was a fine cook! We introduced the Popes to the Pratt Greens and Peter set some of Fred's poems. We also made music together and put on small intimate concerts in Norwich's Assembly Rooms, St Peter Mancroft Church, St George's Tombland and, not surprisingly, St Giles Church. In most of these, compositions by Peter and some of my own featured. He had written Isabel a song for soprano voice, a setting of 'I love all beauteous things' by Robert Bridges, and for me an organ piece *Elegy* in addition to many other songs and instrumental pieces which included *Slackwater Stillness* by Fred Pratt Green. His songs and chamber works lay undiscovered until 2011 when Classicfm magazine of that year declared Peter to be a genius of English song.

Peter died in 1991 in a care home near Ledbury in Herefordshire and a memorial service was held in a nearby village church for which I played the organ. Members of Peter and Noreen's family, and others performed some of his music. In 2010 Ann Martin-Davis and Susan Legg released the CD *Heaven-Haven – the songs of Peter Pope.*

Off the beaten track

Most of the things I have engaged in I have considered to be worthwhile and fruitful. However, there was one episode which, whilst being very interesting, was probably futile and I rather sensed this at the time but nonetheless entered into it wholeheartedly.

In 1980 I saw in *The Musical Times* a notice inviting people to submit to The Chroma Foundation in Montreux, Switzerland, a system for writing down music which might in some way contribute to the eventual replacement of the accepted notation system composers have been using since the time of Guido of Arezzo. Like the alphabetic system used for writing the English language, which is often incongruous in the way words have to be spelt, the standard music notation system also throws up incongruities, none more obvious than when trying to write a whole tone scale. Why can't each spoken sound have its own unique symbol? (That's what George Bernard Shaw wondered.) Why can't musical intervals look like what they sound like?

With this in mind I devised a simple system and on New Year's Eve 1980 sent it off to Switzerland. I heard no more until 1983 when I was informed that my system was to be included alongside those of other inventors in a collection published by Edition Chroma. Soon after its appearance I was invited by Tom Reid of Kirksville, USA, to help form an organisation for the furtherance of the search for a new notation system which would be universally taken up. (Tom was also an Esperantist and how many people speak Esperanto?) Tom had quite a list of other interested parties from all over the world whom he wanted to form into a properly structured organisation with rules, procedures and conditions and all the other paraphernalia of a corporate body, including a treasurer. First he needed a name for the organisation and, by contacting all of us by post, collated a range of suggestions and by process of elimination after due consultation concluded that the most suitable name was Music Notation Modernisation Association, MNMA for short. By a similar process the group chose a logo and then Tom decided there ought to be a chairman. Biographical details of all the members were circulated and by a process of elimination, all done by voting by post, I was elected. And so there I was, the first ever worldwide chairman of the MNMA! What was I supposed to do?

What did occur to me was that none of the members of the Association had ever met and so I decided to hold a conference in Norwich. After enquiries it was decided to use the facilities of the University of East Anglia where there were residential facilities and rooms in which to hold presentations and discussions. This was eagerly taken up and twenty-five delegates signed up for the conference.

The day prior to the commencement of the conference Isabel and I and Tom and Mabel Reid were all crossing the Atlantic in separate aeroplanes at more or less the same time and so at the start of proceedings the next day we were all equally jet-lagged. Delegates attended from the UK, Canada, France, Switzerland, Hong Kong, South Africa, Italy, The Netherlands and Austria and each one had something to contribute regarding the simplification of the practice of music by making it easier to read. There was one innovation which supposedly made it easier to perform keyboard music, a 'six-six' keyboard in which the white keys were tuned to the whole tone scale and the black keys the same but half a tone higher meaning that a chromatic scale could be played simply by playing up the octave white, black, white, black etc. These were all fascinating but overlooked the problem of the millions of keyboards, pianos, organs and the like which were already in existence. Similarly, devising a system using colours to get children to play the required notes is all very well but at some stage there will remain the necessity to learn the conventional system in order to explore the vast repertoire of keyboard music.

On the last evening everyone attended an organ recital in Norwich Cathedral by Dr Arthur Wills which, interestingly enough, included one of his own pieces with an aleatoric section which was of great interest to the delegates as the composer showed everyone the score afterwards.

They were an interesting bunch and all gelled very nicely during the four days of the conference except for one Italian gentleman who managed to make the simplest arrangements complicated to the point of impossibility. There were four people from Italy and the person in question, who had not paid any dues, seemed to be promoting himself as the head of the Italian delegation, much to the annoyance of the other three. In fact technically he was not a member at all. After the conference he and I exchanged letters which increased in acrimony, and from this, my final one to him, you will gather that he was not the easiest of characters:

Dear Muci,

I am indeed sorry that you have such a bad impression of our first conference. The other Italian delegates most certainly did not share your views.

The conference room was small but was a preferable alternative to having twenty-six people in an enormous room and it was not easy to know how many would attend the conference. Indeed the numbers that would attend from Italy fluctuated almost weekly. If you would care to look back over your several letters you cannot fail to recognise how totally confused we were right up to the last as regards who actually was coming from Italy. If you have this to contend with when you organise a conference in Italy then you will have my sympathy and admiration if you manage in achieving anything.

Furthermore, the Association has its own approved letter heading and it is completely out of order for you to appoint yourself head of any division of this Association and correspond on headed notepaper which is not approved by it.

Your speech was of such length and complexity that it exceeded the duration of your cassette. In any event, any English delegate to a conference in Italy would either deliver his speech in Italian or supply transcripts of it even if it were delivered in English. This would be considered good manners and was the practice observed by Prof. Tedde and Prof. Robotti...but not by you.

The business of the £10 is much simpler than you depict. The Association received £10 less than was due to it from you in Conference fees. If you wish to correct this then you may send the outstanding money to me or Bob Stuckey. What it cost you to attend Norwich is very much your own domestic affair. Some came from the USA, South Africa and were very glad that they did, and their expenses must have been enormous.

Your absence from the evening of entertainment was regretted and would have been an ideal opportunity for you to improvise, as others did. Your arrival in the middle of 'Blossom Time' was regrettable and may have been thought by some to be ill mannered...so no lectures on manners please.

Your patriotism is admirable but your belief that Italy is the centre of the universe, all musical inspiration and savoir-faire could, I suspect be challenged without much difficulty.

I sincerely hope that we will meet again at future conferences

and send you my warmest greetings despite the fact that you
alone caused me more headaches than the whole of the rest of
the Conference put together.

Yours sincerely,
RW

Soon after this I received my letter back on which Sgnr Muci
had typed words to the effect that I needed to see a psychiatrist
and be admitted to a lunatic asylum.

At the end of the conference everyone went their separate ways,
never, as far as I know, ever to meet again. One, Richard Parncutt,
an Australian musicologist, sat on the stairs of our house very
undecided as to whether to go to Munich or Armadale (in NSW).
We were never sure where he did go. There never was a second
conference and activity dwindled to a halt after only a few more
years which really came as no surprise to me. As regards musical
notation, nothing has changed though it may have evolved a little
which is, after all, what it has always done.

In 1991 there came into my life a young Chilean man, Patricio
Solar, who wanted to play well-known classical pieces on two types
of Chilean pipes, the Kena and the Sampoña, and he asked me
to make arrangements of particular pieces. The outcome of this
was that we gave two concerts. On 4th May 1991 the audience in
St Gregory's Church, Norwich was treated to 'The sound of the
Andes in Classical music' which included pieces by Bach, Handel,
Mozart, Charpentier, Albinoni alongside Bolivian folksongs and
renaissance dances. This redundant church was cold and somewhat
run down but the acoustics were wonderful and both instrumental
and choral music sounded brilliant within its walls. (In fact I
used St Gregory's for choral concerts when Sine Nomine were
entertaining the Herrenhäuser Chorgemeinschaft of Hanover,
and Oriana from Rouen.) St Gregory's housed an organ which

was well past its best mechanically and extremely awkward to play, but it sounded divine. The same concert was given a few weeks later at Blythburgh church, another stunning venue often used by Benjamin Britten. And that was that. Patricio had a German wife and before very long went back to Germany and I heard nothing more of him. It had been an interesting episode with some novel and enjoyable music making. It was certainly different.

Meanwhile I continued with my choir work and organ playing which brought me a somewhat unusual request for my services. Over the years I have played for innumerable weddings and funerals, most of them unremarkable if one ignores a wedding at which the groom vomited from an upright position just as he was to make his vows; another who, unknown to him, had HE painted in white on the sole of his left foot and LP on the right one which spelled out a plaintive plea as he knelt at the high altar; in the days when the bride wearing white was a sign of purity, a wedding at which the bride wore blue and the groom – a white suit. I have also had requests for some unusual pieces to be played at various points during the ceremony. 'A Whiter Shade of Pale' cropped up quite a lot and for one bridal entry I was asked to play 'The Long March' by Vangelis, which I did not know. I asked if there were a score but was offered a recording from which I transcribed it for use.

Involvement in one memorable wedding began thus; the telephone rang and when I answered it I heard a very obviously American voice saying, 'Mr Watson?'

'Yes.'

'Do you play the organ?'

'Yes.'

'Can you play the wide-door toccata?'

'Yes, I can play the VEE-dor toccata.'

'Would you be available on (date) to play for my daughter's wedding?'

'Yes, I am free on that day. Where is the wedding?'

A village some miles from Norwich was identified.

'Do they have their own organist?'

'Yes, but we don't like him, he plays in gloves.'

'I think we should meet to discuss the arrangement and the music.'

A date was fixed and an address disclosed at which I could meet the USAF Colonel, a short bald man who bore an uncanny resemblance to the *Daily Sketch* cartoon character, Pop.

At the appointed time Isabel and I presented ourselves at the Colonel's front door. It was answered by his wife who invited us in. Embarrassingly, the Colonel addressed his meek spouse as though he were addressing the lowest ranking of his charges.

'Now this wide-door toccata, how does it go? Can you hum it?'

I replied that I would find it difficult to hum the Widor Toccata but suggested that, if they had instrument handy I could give some impression of it. 'Don't just stand there, get the keyboard,' he bellowed at his wife who scuttled away and returned with a very small electronic device of no more than two octaves. I pointed out this this particular instrument would not give a realistic impression of the famous toccata.

'I know,' he announced, 'we'll go over to the church and you can play it there.' And so we did and so I did.

'My daughter also wants "Jerusalem", can you play "Jerusalem"?'

I reassured him on that matter.

'Jerusalem, Jerusalem', he began to sing the well known chorus from Stephen Adams, 'The Holy City', 'Hark, how the angels sing.'

'Why she wants that I don't know,' he muttered.

'I don't think she means THAT "Jerusalem",' I explained.

'You mean there's another "Jerusalem"?!'

'Yes,' I assured him and reminded him of the Parry setting.

'Oh, no!' he retorted. 'Not the dark Satanic mills!'

And so we returned to the house where his wife was dispatched to the kitchen to make us a cup of tea.

All matters having been discussed and agreed regarding my playing for the wedding, we returned home and to our surprise received within a few days a beautifully printed invitation to the wedding reception. This turned out to be a very splendid affair which included, amongst other delights, pink champagne for the ladies, all the comestibles having been flown in from the United States via the PX.

Sine Nomine were also often invited to sing at weddings, two in particular come to mind a few days apart. The first was for a rather well-off and spoiled young lady who had everyone running around in circles and for whose wedding no expense had been spared. She was a little tiddly on the day! The second in complete contrast was of a young woman in her terminal illness who hardly had the strength to get to the church and walk up the aisle. She did arrive quite late and in the time of waiting we were all wondering if she would make it at all. When she uttered the words 'till death us do part' no one could disguise the lump in the throat. Such bravery; within a very few weeks she died.

The Norfolk Organists' Association

Within the first few months of arriving in Norwich I had joined what was then the Norfolk Guild of Organists which in 1998 changed its title to the Norfolk Organists' Association. There isn't, as far as I know, a collective noun for organ enthusiasts but a 'mixture' seems like a good one to me. What a mixture an organists' association is! The players (and they aren't all players) range from the virtuoso to the onlysoso. The non-players range from those who can do wonders with a screwdriver to the those who can tell you the wind pressure on the Sesquialtera II in Trier Cathedral. The Norfolk Organists' Association endeavours to cater for all tastes.

I have served on its committee and enjoyed one term of office as Chairman. Until the summer of 1992 Ralph Bootman produced the quarterly Newsletter which dealt primarily with notifications of what the Guild was doing and what was going on in the realms of organ building and maintenance locally. After producing a staggering 100 of these, Ralph bowed out and I volunteered to take up the baton. My first edition was still titled *The Newsletter* but after that I renamed it *The NGO (or NOA) Journal*. I also sought to broaden the scope of what was covered in the publication by inviting articles on any aspects of an organist's experience. The Journal would keep the membership informed about the organisation's activities but would also be a platform for articles not only about organs, but church music, church musicians and associated topics. Over the years I have solicited articles from Dr Francis Jackson, Dr Roy Massey, Dr Gerald Gifford, Professor Peter Aston, Canon Michael Perham who was at the time Precentor of Norwich Cathedral and later became Bishop of Gloucester, the composer Diana Burrell, daughter of Bernard Burrell, assistant organist at Norwich Cathedral under Heathcote Statham and Bryan Runnett to name but a few. However, the most credit for Journal fodder must go to the membership who have sent in articles on an incredible range of topics. From all of these articles I have learned a great deal.

Over the years one member in particular, Pauline Stratton, has fed in numerous articles of historic interest which she meticulously researches mainly from the archives of local newspapers. Her collected articles would make a fascinating publication in its own right. And I have to admit that *The NGO Journal* has also been a platform for some of my own views on things spurred on by the view that an editor who is not opinionated isn't worth his salt; I have been and still am opinionated as any who read some of my editorials and articles will have discovered.

Another regular event in the calendar of the NOA has been their version of *Desert Island Discs*. This was initiated by Ken Smith whose first castaway was Professor Peter Aston, with Ken taking the role of Roy Plomley (Sue Lawley, Kirsty Young or whoever). Ken's castaways included David Dunnett, Katherine Dienes and yours truly (his last). Ken brought great energy and originality to Guild activities, another of which was as quiz-master at another of the Guild's regular events, the Quiz and Chips evening. When ill-health forced him to curtail his active involvement in the Guild I came to the rescue again and took on the continuance of *Desert Island Discs*. Here again I have learned such a great deal from interviewing people about their lifetime's experiences. Many amusing and surprising things have come to light in the course of such encounters. Tales of a Precentor of Norwich Cathedral holding up an Italian train by standing in front of it and of an eminent cathedral organist and recitalist being threatened with court proceedings if he didn't stop practising, have brought amusement and entertainment to Association members over the years. On one occasion the scheduled castaway, the Precentor of Norwich Cathedral who was also at the time acting Dean, was required at short notice to attend an important meeting in another part of the country. Bravely the then current Chairman of the Association, Martin Cottam stepped into the breach at less than a day's notice and he too had some engaging tales to tell of his life's journey; even the most humble of us have stories worth hearing. This mention of Martin Cottam cannot be allowed to pass without reference to his outstanding skills as an illustrator which are currently features of the *Organists' Review*. Alongside this, his knowledge of and enthusiasm for organs is unparalleled and to the great benefit of the Association he is particularly skilled at devising and arranging organ crawls in the city and county and further afield, even venturing as far afield as Holland.

Two other castaways with fascinating tales to tell were Peter Stevenson and Kenneth Ryder. Peter, a Norfolk-born musician was a pupil of Heathcote Statham and for a short time was organist at Portsmouth Cathedral. But his main career was in Hong Kong where he contributed significantly to the music in that fascinating city. Returning to Norfolk in retirement, he continued to make a noteworthy contribution to music in the area as organist, recitalist and teacher, his final post being at Princes Street United Reformed Church in Norwich where he staged regular lunchtime concerts. Kenneth Ryder was the Organist at St Peter Mancroft in Norwich for forty-two years where he oversaw the installation of the Peter Collins instrument. A gifted player himself, his main contribution to the church music in the area was as a teacher. He died at the young age of sixty-six, little over one year into his retirement.

One of the most poignant *Desert Island* events involved the recently-appointed Master of the Music at Norwich Cathedral, Ashley Grote. Despite his mere thirty years, the account of his progress to the highest echelons of church music was full of interest and fascination. Surprisingly, he did not avoid talking about his domestic difficulties since moving to Norwich and the emotionally draining sequence of events surrounding his four-year-old daughter Emily's treatment for a brain tumour which involved her being in the United States for twelve weeks. Ashley's gratitude to the Great Ormond Street Hospital where Emily was first treated prompted him to run the 2015 London Marathon in support of their work. He completed the course in under four hours and raised close to £20,000. All of this and his recent remarriage along with his superlative musicianship both as organist and choir director have earned him the affection of the Norwich Cathedral congregation and other musicians in the region. Ashley is the latest in a long line of superb musicians I have had the privilege of knowing throughout my musical journey.

The Association stages a full and varied annual programme of events and works very hard to stimulate interest in the organ and its music. Mention must be made here of Mathew Martin, certainly one of the most tireless promoters of the organ and its music in the locality. During his tenure of the post of Organist and Choirmaster at St Thomas's Church, Heigham, he staged an annual concert series for several years providing a platform to a wide variety of instrumentalists and ensembles and attracting leading organ recitalists to play the fine two manual EW Storr organ in the church of which there have been two recordings by James Parsons.

Free Agent

I was in post for twenty-two years at St Giles Church, Norwich and I accompanied services there which were 'higher' than those held at the Roman Catholic Cathedral, a mere two hundred yards away. I sang 'the Propers' as part of the Mass on Sunday mornings which ended with the Angelus, and Evensong was followed by a healing service and Benediction complete with Monstrance and full bells and smells.

Whilst in post there I arranged several concerts in the church in aid of its restoration fund. When a considerable sum of money was needed to make the tower safe I composed a hymn, words and music for use occasionally in order to invoke the help of the Almighty in saving this city landmark. The words never found any further use but the tune *Restoration* found its way into a book of hymns in the USA.

My departure from St Giles was unceremonious and swift. I had been displeased with one breach of incumbent/organist etiquette but chose not to make an issue of it. But one Sunday morning in 1991 I went to the church and played for the morning Eucharist and within three hours had typed out my resignation and put it through the letterbox of the Vicar's front door. Only a few weeks earlier he and I had demolished the best part of a bottle of Isle of Jura single malt whiskey and agreed certain principles regarding the direction of the music in the church. On that particular Sunday morning, with his blessing, some very unworthy music-making took place during the service of which I had no prior knowledge, all of which flew in the face of the principles he and I had agreed.

What a blessing in disguise this turned out to be as my departure from St Giles led to us starting to attend Norwich Cathedral, one of the truly pivotal things I think I have ever done. Worshipping at Norwich Cathedral is totally uplifting. One has the confidence that every aspect of a service will be impeccably done and very rarely is that not the case. The most likely times when things will fall below expectations are during choir holidays when visiting choirs and organists are pulled in to fill the gap. These can be uncomfortable experiences if the visiting choir is simply not up to it or the visiting organist can't contain his exuberance at being at one of the largest consoles in the country and opts for playing over each tune on the Tuba.

Very occasionally however, despite the totally professional approach of all concerned in the worship, does something go wrong when the home team are there. I remember one Palm Sunday that got off to a very shaky start. On Palm Sunday the Eucharist begins outside the west end of the cathedral and most of the congregation gather there and are given greenery to wave as the procession moves into the building. A hymn is begun outside and the choir enter the cathedral singing it, followed by the worshippers. On one memorable occasion the hymn was to be 'Ride on, ride on in majesty' to the tune *St Drostane*, the first three notes of which are the same as for *Winchester New*, the more frequently used and possibly the more familiar tune. The hymn is begun unaccompanied, the organ not joining in until the cross and lights have entered through the west doors. Those within the building, who for whatever reason had chosen not to begin the service outside, had heard the hymn start in the distance and had started to sing it to the tune *Winchester New*. As the choir processed down the nave the two tunes could be heard simultaneously and with the organ virtually at full stretch one would have imagined that *St Drostane* would eventually prevail. Not so. That section of the congregation singing *Winchester New* stuck to their guns and so it continued to the end of the hymn; they probably thought the choir were singing a descant!

At a fund-raising concert which involved a brass band, those present were treated to a an enjoyable variety of music. The climax of the concert was to be a performance of the *Toccata* from Boëllmann's *Suite Gothique* arranged for brass band with the organ joining in at the point where the main theme returns played in pedal octaves. When the great moment came, the organ joined in (presumably in C minor) which immediately highlighted the fact that the band was in a different key. This became immediately obvious and the organ stopped playing instantly and left the rest of the piece to the band.

Dame Gillian Wier was the celebrity recitalist in one of the summer evening Norfolk & Norwich Festival recitals and had chosen to play Nielsen's *Commodio,* a rather long piece, and had got to about the halfway point when one of the louder stops developed a persistent cipher. It was clear that this had to be dealt with before the piece could continue and so Dame Gillian found a cadence and stopped playing. Fortunately in the audience was a local organ builder, Richard Bower, who, with the note still sounding, scuttled up to see what he could do. After a few minutes the noise stopped and it appeared that the cipher had been cured. Not so. Dame Gillian appeared on the screen holding up the offending pipe for all to see, which brought a spontaneous round of applause. The Nielsen was resumed where she had left off.

Norwich Cathedral holds popular organ recitals on Bank Holidays and in 2002 David Dunnett asked me to play the Bank Holiday recital which on this occasion fell on a Tuesday as it was the additional holiday in celebration of the Queen's Golden Jubilee. David was in Rome with the Cathedral Choir. On the evening prior to my recital a ceremony took place in the Cathedral Close in which a beacon was lit. Having attended this, I went into the organ loft, switched the organ on and checked that all my piston settings were as I had left them. All was well. On the Tuesday morning I arrived at the console about twenty minutes before the recital was scheduled to start and pressed the power switches. Nothing happened. The instrument was dead. There was no possibility of getting the tuner there in time and the Cathedral was filling up. Only a few minutes before 11 o'clock did the duty Canon announce to the assembled gathering that there would be no recital and so they all went away. As a consolation David put me down for the 2003 New Year's Day recital instead, which went off without a hitch and which required only two changes to my programme. I was able to replace Herbert Murrill's transcription of Walton's *Crown Imperial* which had been appropriate for the original recital (the only reason it was included as I am not wild about transcriptions and find this Walton piece far too repetitive). I replaced it with three of Flor Peeters's *Ten Chorales Op. 39,* which I felt, and still feel to be unjustifiably neglected.

En passant

Once when on holiday in Northern France we found ourselves quite near Grez-sur-Loing where Delius lived at the latter part of his life. An enquiry at the Mairie disclosed the location of the house and the fact that it was privately owned and occupied. Also disclosed was that the occupant may well be amenable to showing us round, and so we knocked on the front door. It was answered by a young Filipino man having difficulty speaking French. Once it became apparent that we were English, communication became much easier. Indeed the very old Madame D'Aubigny preferred to speak English as, having come from good stock in Russia, she had been brought up by English governesses. We were welcomed with great enthusiasm and were offered tea over which she told us of the many English visitors that had dropped by over the years, some very famous musicians among them. We also learned much of Delius's life in the house and were then allowed to wander at will, even into the bedroom where he had died. We were shown where Delius had worked with Eric Fenby, the Scarborough organist who had become the composer's amanuensis and were also invited to walk down the garden at the bottom of which flows the River Loing, and a more idyllic setting cannot be imagined. This was indeed a walk in a paradise garden. (What a pity *The Paradise Garden* in Delius's opera *A village Romeo and Juliet* is a pub!) Not far from the house is the church where Eric Fenby would go, much to the annoyance of the agnostic Delius, so we had a look in there too.

There is something other-worldly about being in locations where creative geniuses have lived and worked. I suppose that for a composer of lesser standing there might be the vain hope that, simply in being where they were, some of their creativity might rub off!

On the same jaunt we found ourselves exploring the delightful city of Dijon. Wandering into the church of Notre-Dame, we saw, pinned to the wall, a typewritten note to the effect that Léon Boëllman had written his *Suite Gothique* for the Ghys organ in the church, which was, as we were reading, being played. The young French recitalist Thierry Mechler was rehearsing for a recital but didn't seem to mind us introducing ourselves and showing the organ to us. It is a surprisingly modest affair. Thierry Mechler and I exchanged addresses and on my return home I sent him a copy of *Toccata* which, some months later he let me know that he was playing.

Some years later a short holiday in Honfleur threw up something of a surprise. We had been unaware of any musical connections with Honfleur until we discovered that the eccentric composer Erik Satie had lived in the town. A visit to his former residence, now a museum, was, apart from being an interesting one, also a highly amusing and sometimes bizarre experience. Satie's eccentricities didn't only manifest themselves in music but in drawings, writings and gadgetry. In one room is a strange 'magic roundabout' which visitors operate by sitting on a bicycle seat and pedalling. As one makes a circuit, a central umbrella opens and closes, lights brighten and dim and bizarre instruments can be seen suspended in the centre. In another room there is a display of jottings in Satie's hand, both musical and otherwise, and a video presentation in which prominent French musicians, including Poulenc and Nadia Boulanger, discuss the merits of Satie's music. The logos for the whole exhibition and notices on doors are in the shape of a pear alluding to one of his pieces 'en forme de poire'.

Back in Paris we attended a recital by Olivier Latry in Notre Dame. It was, needless to say, first class but we were surprised by the poor standard of English which had been attempted in the programme notes. Before the recital began we were approached by two Japanese members of the audience and asked if we were English and could we explain the programme notes. Our response was, yes, we were English and we didn't understand them either! Here is a sample: *A half failure by obtaining only a second prize of organ makes his (César Franck's) father did not make it possible him to persevere in the studies of organ. It is however in contact with the organ that is built all the career of César Franck under the double activity of concert performer and servant of the worship.* On our return home Isabel felt moved to write and express her surprise to Olivier Latry that there was no one connected with that most prestigious of cathedrals who could produce programme notes in comprehensible English and that this did not reflect well on Notre Dame. Latry had the courtesy to reply and in his very pleasant letter pointed out that the production of programmes and their content was not his responsibility.

Visiting friends near Tampere in Finland provided the opportunity to visit Ainola, the house of Sibelius, still as it was when Sibelius occupied it, his study complete with writing desk, pens, his white jacket and walking sticks. At the end of the garden is Sibelius's grave set among trees, and standing near to it one could easily imagine a flight of swans passing overhead such as inspired the evocative final movement of his fifth symphony.

Further afield in Russia whilst staying in Yalta, there was the possibility to visit the house of Chekov. The White Dacha, as it is known, was a magnet for artists, authors and musicians, particularly Rachmaninov and Chaliapin. It houses an upright piano which would have been played by Rachmaninov.

In 2001 we marked our retirement by taking a trip all the way around the world. Our first destination was Hong Kong where we spent four days. One morning when strolling through the city's streets, we were fascinated by a display of strange-looking oriental musical instruments in a shop window. Exploration inside was an essential. The store had on display an incredible range of musical instruments of every sort, stringed, wind, percussion, and pianos in every size from the full concert grand to the neat upright. As we browsed, one of the sales assistants was picking out a tune on a piano and more curiously, even though the man could obviously not play, he was picking out a tune on the white notes which was perfectly pentatonic. I was fascinated, and an attempt to express and explain my fascination to him resulted in him finding me a plastic stool and insisting that I play something. And so I played Scarlatti's *C major Sonata K159*. When I had done, all the sales assistants within earshot burst into spontaneous applause, grinning and bowing in a most engaging way. I don't know to what extent they understood English or identified with Western music but I came away feeling that once again music had crossed barriers that other languages had created. They offered me a regular job!

From Hong Kong we flew to Perth in Australia where we attended the morning Eucharist and where I was allowed a few minutes at the console. However, the focal point in Australia was Melbourne where we would stay with June Nixon and her husband Neville. Here I would enjoy playing the superb T C Lewis organ in St Paul's Cathedral and give a lunchtime recital there. There is one building in Melbourne which is unmissable for any Yorkshireman, Captain Cook's birthplace. This small stone dwelling was originally situated at Marton on the outskirts of Middlesbrough but in 1933 was dismantled stone by stone and shipped out to Australia and is now open to visitors in Melbourne's Fitzroy Gardens. Before leaving Melbourne in our hired car, we visited the Melbourne University Grainger Museum which houses exhibits which highlight the composer's inventive traits. Some of the devices he assembled have to be seen to be believed.

And so to Sydney and the Cathedral. At the Eucharist we heard the Cathedral Singers directed by Michael Deasey who told me that he had once brought a choir to Norwich in the days of Michael Nicholas. At the organ was Mark Quarmby, one of only two MQs in the Royal College of Organists, the other being Miles Quick who was for several years at Norwich School. Mark told me how easy it was to get access to the Sydney Town Hall organ and gave me a telephone number to ring. This I did and was told that all I had to do was to turn up at the Town Hall and tell them I had come to play the organ and get the keys from the reception desk. The keys as it happened were already in the hands of Manuel, the organ tuner. As I entered the hall I was asked by a lady if I was going to play the organ. The fact that I was filled her with joy as she owned a recording of the organ played by Marcel Dupré and had always wanted to hear it live. My arrival at the console coincided with the emergence from a panel in the organ case of Manuel. I was free to play and so worked my way through the pistons towards full organ and drawing the 64' Pedal Contra Trombone. I could see through the mirror that a small audience had formed and so I launched into *The War March of the Priests* being something I thought they would recognise.

The playing over I prepared to leave but was then invited with Isabel to have a look inside the organ so in we went through the door in the panelling. Inside, Manuel had an office and a workshop complete with tea-making facilities. He led us to the foot of the largest pipe and if he had had his way would have had us climbing ladders and walking along gangways, but we had other things to see and do, so thanked him and took our leave.

Next we flew to Christchurch to begin a four-week visit to New Zealand, two weeks in the South Island and two in the North Island. At the time Katherine Dienes, a native of New Zealand, was Assistant Organist at Norwich Cathedral and one evening prior to our departure she and her husband Patrick ate with us at Roseberry Cottage and helped us work out routes around the two islands which, as it turned out, we followed to the letter. It was all spot-on (particularly the recommendation to have a pizza in The One Red Dog in Wellington). We did encounter organs in the major towns and cities but the most significant event while we were there was in Auckland where we learned that my younger daughter had given birth to my first (and only) grandson. We lit a candle for him in Auckland Cathedral.

The following year we crossed Canada by train. Toronto, where we stayed with Elizabeth Shepherd, proved to be musically interesting on various fronts. On one evening we were joined for the evening meal by a neighbour of Elizabeth's, a retired opera singer, Roxolana Roslak who had sung at Covent Garden and who had been the last person with whom Glenn Gould had had a relationship. Following TV appearances with Gould in 1975 they had recorded Hindemith's *Das Marienleben*.

Through another contact of Elizabeth's, we met Patricia and William Wright. Patricia had succeeded Melville Cook as organist at the Metropolitan United Church in Toronto which is home to the largest pipe organ in Canada and thanks to her I had some time at the console. A portrait of Melville Cook who had emigrated to Canada in 1966, hangs in the vestry. Another significant 'hands-on' experience was playing the organ in the church of St Mary Magdalene where Healey Willan had been in post. Fittingly, I played two pieces by Willan, which may well have been played on that very organ, perhaps by Willan himself.

The final organ encounter in Toronto was in Casa Loma, a museum that was once the mansion residence of the wealthy financier Sir Henry Mill Pellatt. The mansion houses a mighty Wurlitzer organ into the workings of which one can peer as one ascends from floor to floor. The $75,000 instrument, built in New

York, arrived just in time to be auctioned off to pay Pellatt's tax debt. It was purchased for $40. The organ is maintained by the Toronto Theatre Organ Society and is used four times a year for concerts and twice a year to accompany silent films.

Whilst we were in Canada we also learned that my short anthem, *If there is to be peace* with words by Lao Tsu was to be used on 7th July in a Memorial Service for The British Commonwealth Ex-Services League at The Cenotaph directed by Peter Halliday, and to feature in the Royal British Legion Festival of Remembrance in the Royal Albert Hall. Herein lies one of a few disappointments in my publishing experience in that it is not mentioned as such in the Festival booklet. It was sung at the end when the poppies were floating downward and appears in the programme simply as 'Anthem'.

There were poignant moments during a trip to Israel. During a boat trip on the Sea of Galilee a young Israeli violinist played while we sang 'Dear Lord and Father of Mankind'; singing the words 'Sabbath rest by Galilee' reduced some of the party to tears. Later at a Son et Lumière presentation in the King David Citadel, the finale was a projection on the ancient walls of the words 'O Pray for the Peace of Jerusalem', which brought to mind the final section of Parry's anthem, *I was glad*. Standing in the Garden of Gethsemane with the city of Jerusalem in full view, Bairstow's setting of *The Lamentations* came to mind; 'Jerusalem, Jerusalem, return unto the Lord your God'. In complete contrast, I have to admit that floating on my back in the Dead Sea was without any musical associations!

In December 2006 to mark our twentieth wedding anniversary Isabel and I took ourselves off to Budapest. Budapest is a musician's paradise. So many great musicians have associations with it, particularly the Opera House. We attended a performance of *The Nutcracker* there and imagined Mahler and other famous composers and conductors on the rostrum. We saw a production of *Nabucco* in a second opera house and visited Liszt's apartment which houses pianos, including an ornate Chickering, and other Liszt memorabilia and where the walls are hung with portraits of Chopin, Schumann and other Liszt contemporaries. A short walk away is Kodaly's apartment where some of his manuscripts were on display, some choral pieces we recognised as having sung.

However, as it was near Christmas, we decided to go to a carol concert we had seen advertised in the St Stephen's Basilica to be given by the Gabrieli Choir. This was something of an eye-opener as the concert could easily have been in an English chapel, featuring, as it did several well-known carols by English composers. The standard of performance was exemplary, every bit as good as King's. As we left the building we hovered in order to meet the conductor Richárd Solyóm with whom we had a short conversation in fluent English, not surprising as it transpired that Richard who is half English and half Hungarian sang for some years as a lay clerk in Carlisle Cathedral and is totally au fait with the English choral repertoire. Here was an opportunity not to be missed. Having taken a note of his postal address, on my return home I sent him some of my vocal settings. One in particular caught his interest because of its Lake District associations, my *Shepherd's Carol,* setting words by the Cumbrian poet Norman Nicholson. I was delighted to learn some months later that Richard planned to include this carol in the concert the following year. And then in 2009 he would be bringing the Gabrieli Choir on an English tour and performing the carol in the church of St Kentigern, Keswick. We treated ourselves to a couple of days in the Lake District to go to hear the concert. I took with me a copy of *Toccata* which I gave to their organist Gesztesi-Toth László and in October 2011 he included it in a concert in the Anglican Church in Budapest. On such occasions I am reminded of one piece of advice given to me by Bill Elkin that day in Salhouse, to the effect that part of a publisher's job (and presumably a composer's!) is to give music away.

In 2006 I celebrated my seventieth birthday and the highlight was a composite recital in Norwich Cathedral organised primarily by Gordon Barker with no small input from Isabel and David Dunnett. A large number of family and friends gathered in the Cathedral. The evening began with Gillian Ward Russell playing *Excursion*, a piece I had written for her. Tim Patient then played four of my hymn preludes on *All things Bright and Beautiful, Aberystwyth, O Waly waly* and *East Acklam*. This was followed by Dr Arthur Wills who played his own *Adoro Te devote*, commissioned for me by Gordon and Celia. (Arthur later referred to this in his autobiography, *Full with Wills*, but unfortunately got my name muddled up with that of Gordon and reports having attended 'Ron Barker's seventieth birthday!') David Dunnett then played *Toccata* followed by *Badinage* and ended with a complete performance of *Sonatina*. David directed a lusty performance of 'Happy Birthday Herr Bach', with appropriate words and a musical tribute by Dr June Nixon in the form of amusing words to one of her organ pieces, a trio on *Ellacombe*. After this we all moved into the Cathedral's newly opened and award-winning Refectory for refreshments. I was very touched and delighted to find there to my surprise that Kate and Mike Turver had come all the way from Guisborough for the occasion.

Gordon Barker had arrived in Mattishall in 2000 and we immediately became good friends. Gordon is an organist of considerable experience at Parish Church level and knows the church music repertoire inside out. Several of my compositions have been influenced by him and his approbation has always been encouraging. One of my most successful pieces *Badinage* is dedicated to him.

The year after my seventieth birthday it was to be Gordon's seventieth birthday. Unlike myself, Gordon loathes surprises. One of Gordon and Celia's grandsons was at that time a chorister in the Canterbury Cathedral choir and it was the intention of the whole family to go to Evensong on the Sunday that was Gordon's birthday. I decided that I would like to write an anthem for Gordon based on a hymn that had a particular significance for him and that could be used in that service with their grandson Matthew as the treble soloist. I consulted Celia to find out which this might be and discovered that they had had 'Angel Voices ever singing' at their wedding. When the anthem was complete I sent a copy of *Voces Angelorum* to Gordon and Celia's son, who would show it to David Flood and ask him if he would consider using it as the anthem on that particular day. The news that David Flood was willing to do this gave me great satisfaction and much pleasure added to by the fact that he purchased a set of scores for Canterbury Cathedral.

As it turned out this could never have been kept a secret for very long as the title of the anthem appeared on the published music list, but we managed to conceal this from Gordon until the morning of his birthday when, over breakfast I presented him with the score. Needless to say the Cathedral Choir gave an exemplary performance of the piece but there was to be one disappointment in that, on the day, Matthew had a croaky voice because of a cold and could not sing the solo. The boy who did sing the solo, however, was superb. (Aren't they all?)

I had slightly less luck a year later with a piece I wrote for my friend Alan Barber's eightieth birthday. Alan's brother George runs a very competent choir in Stockton-on-Tees and they deputise in Durham Cathedral from time to time with Alan as organist. My plan was to have James Lancelot include the piece *Eucharistia* (Celebration) as the voluntary at an Evensong which it would be contrived to get Alan to attend. However, the go-between, George, was unable to convince James Lancelot that this was a viable plan. So I sent Alan the score of the piece as a gift and he decided to play it himself in a recital at St Peter's Church, Stockton-on-Tees on 24th October 2009. *Eucharistia* is not easy and Alan played it brilliantly, indeed his playing throughout the whole recital gave no indication of his advancing years. Happily *Eucharistia* was also taken up by a very gifted organist newly arrived in Aylsham in Norfolk, Harry Macey. Harry spent most his life in the Windsor area, making music of a high standard in all its forms. As he accompanied services in cathedrals I discovered that the piece was getting some very prestigious airings. And not just *Eucharistia*; Harry took to including other pieces of mine in his recitals and so I wrote him *Theme and Variations* and dedicated a revisited anthem, 'He Who Would Valiant Be' to him in token of his choir training skills.

For Francis Jackson's ninetieth birthday I wrote *90 bars*, a musing on the tune York which is exactly 90 bars long. Being aware of Dr Jackson's long and close association with Banks I thought that they might like to publish the piece but I was not aware that they were planning *Fanfare for Francis* which was already well progressed and so I had already missed the boat. Geoffrey Atkinson came to the rescue and published the piece in time for me to send the score to the great man. In a letter of thanks Dr Jackson told me he had already played it in a recital in York where it had been well received.

To mark my seventy-fifth birthday David Dunnett agreed to let me give an organ recital in the Cathedral to a privately invited audience. The recital was programme was made up of pieces which had had a particular significance for me throughout my musical journey: Franck *Choral No. 3*, Bach *Fantasia in C minor BWV 562*, *Jour de Noces* by Harold Maddock, John Gardener's *Hymn-tune Prelude on Down Ampney*, my own *Toccata*, *Toccata* by Francis Jackson, *Elegy* by Peter Pope, *Introduction & Passacaglia* from Sonata no 8 by Rheinberger and *L'Ange à la Trompette* by Jacques Charpentier. As a reward for sitting through my playing, guests were offered a glass of wine in the south transept.

Coda

I'm only a partial organ enthusiast. I think they are amazing pieces of machinery and I understand how they work and I suppose I can tell a Kleis from a Harrison & Harrison. However, when I enter any building where there is a pipe organ, whilst I will always be interested in getting my hands on it and exploring the sounds it makes, I am not remotely interested whether it is tracker or pneumatic or what the wind pressures are, and have no burning desire to go crawling around inside it. (As a member of an organists' organisation I am well aware that the innards of instruments are all that some members are interested in.)

If, on the other hand, the building were to house an electronic instrument I wouldn't bother to look at it at all and certainly would make no attempt to gain permission to play it. All electronic organs leave me cold. Having said that, I do have one at home, a two manuals and pedal instrument which is used extensively, but only for practice and playing over compositions. I derive no pleasure from the sounds it makes; for pleasure I play the piano. I must nevertheless concede that many organists have electronic instruments at home and do derive much pleasure from them. My problem with them is that the sounds they make are imitations and lack that dimension which makes the sound of a pipe organ so satisfying, the physicality of wind passing through a pipe making an attractive sound or making a reed vibrate. I also concede that electronic organs offer more for the money and are portable; didn't Carlo Curley take his on his travels with him? However, I would rather have a real lemon than a plastic replica containing lemon juice! Whenever required to play an electronic organ for a service, I make sure any reverberation device is switched off. Playing something which is pretending to be an organ is one thing; pretending it is in some great Gothic cathedral is a pretence too far!

I suppose that makes me a purist. Fine; I'm also something of a pedant. I declined a Fellowship from a locally invented School of Church Music on the grounds that I had to do absolutely nothing to qualify for it. I could have had an extra string of letters after my name which may have impressed the impressionable but which I knew were meaningless, and I could have had a set of splendid robes. Apart from when directing the choir in a church service, I rarely took the trouble to robe in which case I was content with my simple black gown and very simple ARCO hood which I had worked hard for and which has some standing; a case of less being more, I think.

I also get very hot under the collar about the standards of organ playing which are tolerated, even taken for granted, having attended weddings and funerals at which the playing was dreadful. What bride and groom would not raise merry hell if the food at the reception was virtually inedible, or the flowers wilted or the photographs out of focus? What bride and groom have ever complained because the hymn tune was unrecognisable or played so inaccurately and slowly that no one could sing it? Why don't clergy see it as their responsibility to ensure that the service, and all that happens during it, is to an acceptable standard? Is this not why organ music is now being supplanted by recordings for both weddings and funeral services?

I fully subscribe to the sentiments of Psalm 150 exhorting us to worship God on all available musical instruments. It is a common sight these days to go into churches now and find banks of speakers, rows of music stands and drum sets. Good! But should this mean that the organ is consigned to silence? I am not aware that music groups have very much in their repertoire suitable for use at a funeral and in any event, could they all be assembled at any time during any day to provide music for such a service? There is and will remain for some years to come, the need of organists. But where are they? Organ builders have never been busier and organ recitalists are in considerable demand, but there are many fewer competent church musicians who are willing to take on a regular commitment at parish and village level. Many small churches are without a regular organist and depend on having lists of players who are willing to deputise, from which they will hopefully be able to find someone to cover particular Sundays. The situation is very different from the way it was when I started out and how it will evolve I cannot imagine.

I also believe that there is a great difference between 'amateur' and 'amateurish'. I have heard many performances of music by amateurs, either soloists or ensembles, which achieved the highest standards and thrilled me as a listener equally as much as professionals would have done. Norwich is and has been home to some very fine amateur choirs. For many years Angela Dugdale's Broadland Singers were held in the highest esteem and the Keswick Hall Choir, founded by Geoffrey Laycock, developed by John Aplin and now directed by Chris Duarte turn in highly professional and electrifying performances. (And dare I mention at its best Sine Nomine?) I have no time, however, for the 'amateurish' approach that has as its yardstick 'near enough is good enough'. In my book I'm afraid it isn't.

As a traveller I have learned that there are two types of journey. There are journeys which are made as a means of getting to one's destination as quickly as possible and others where the journey itself is part of the overall experience, with pleasure and interest along the way, and perhaps a little turbulence. Such has been my musical journey. I didn't particularly want to be a quantity surveyor, contracts manager or college lecturer but I did enjoy success and no small amount of pleasure in these roles and, most important, a comfortable and steady income enabling me to indulge my true passion. I am often asked why I didn't pursue a career in music. Well it just didn't turn out that way and besides, I feel I have had the best of music by engaging in it as an amateur. It has been a therapy and the medium in which I could most fluently express myself. I have listened to the music of my choice, directed choral music of my choice, played piano and organ music of my choice and composed music of my choice; what could be better than that! And there can be no greater source of gratification for a composer than to know that his compositions are being used. The arrival of the Performing Right Society's regular printouts serve as comforting evidence that one's pieces are being performed in recitals and are being broadcast here in the UK and in Europe, even downloaded from iTunes!

As a church organist I have heard countless sermons and scriptural readings and two have always chimed with me. The parable of the talents places a responsibility on us all to develop whatever talents we have been blessed with and put them to good use. And when I am parting with complimentary copies of my pieces in the hope that some will be taken up, I am reminded of the parable of the sower. Some will fall on stony ground but hopefully enough will fall on fertile ground to make it all worthwhile.

And so the journey is nearly over, and what a journey it has been with so much fulfilment from the music experienced and the people with whom it has been shared. Of all the pieces which transport me to a higher plane it is English music which has the most profound effect on me, particularly choral music. Harris's *Faire is the heaven*, Stanford's *Magnificat in G* and Sumsion's *They that go down to the sea in ships* leave me speechless.

However, in my young days it seemed that there were some pieces, copies of which were in every organist's music cupboard, Pietro Yon's *Humoresque*, Vaughan Williams' *Rhosymedre*, Parry's *Little Organ Book* to mention only three. 'Wouldn't it be nice,' I would muse, 'if some day there were to be something of mine in every organist's music cupboard.' I wonder if there ever will be, and what it might be.